LEON COUNTY PUBLIC LIBRARY
3 1260 00
S0-CNH-783

JUDGE AND BE DAMNED

The discovery of a dead judge in bizarre circumstances is thought by the police to be connected with a recent trial at which he had presided, but when Linus Rintoul, a government vet, becomes involved with an attractive dog-breeder, he learns that there are unexpected connections between the judge and the breeder. His new friendship leads him into the show ring, where he finds that some people will go to extraordinary lengths both to win and keep other competitors—like Linus—out. Linus refuses to bow to pressure, but he does not realize what he is up against, nor the lengths to which some people will go . . .

JUDGE AND BE DAMNED

Janet Edmonds

A Lythway Book

CHIVERS PRESS
BATH

First published in Great Britain 1990
by
William Collins Sons & Co. Ltd
This Large Print edition published by
Chivers Press
by arrangement with
HarperCollins Publishers
and in the U.S.A. with the author
1992

ISBN 0 7451 1489 X

British Library Cataloguing in Publication Data available

JUDGE AND BE DAMNED

CHAPTER ONE

It was a glorious day. The sort of day when it seemed almost immoral to be paid to drive out into the country and walk across green fields or lean on gates and discuss cows with a knowledgeable cowman. The trouble was, it was all too often not quite like that. There was too frequently a sombre side to the visits of a government vet, as there was on the present occasion. This was Linus Rintoul's second visit to Uppertop Farm in the last three days and he didn't expect to find that the cow had got better. No vet enjoyed diagnosing a notifiable disease in someone's herd but in Tom Brigsteer's case it seemed particularly hard. His small herd of pedigree Gloucesters was possibly the best of the very few left of that breed and under the dour, unsentimental cloak of the efficient modern farmer, they occupied a soft spot in a way that his commercial Friesians never could. Now one of them had gone down with BSE—an essential abbreviation of Bovine Spongiform Encephalopathy, the new disease of cattle which left the brain in holes, like a sponge, and destroyed the animal's co-ordination.

The fields on both sides of the road were a tribute to Tom's efficiency and Linus, in no hurry to spoil a beautiful day any sooner than he had to, pulled over and leant on the steering-wheel, surveying the immediate landscape.

As everywhere on Uppertop, the fences were in good order, the gates securely attached to their gate-posts, hanging high enough to open freely. These days they were chained and padlocked to keep unwelcome visitors away. In the pasture on his left, a trough was clearly visible against the horizon and Linus knew it was fed from its own standpipe and that if he went across to inspect it, it would be full and clean. On the other side of the road a field of oats, not yet plumped out and golden, rustled in the slight breeze, the delicately suspended seed-heads susceptible to the least hint of movement in the air. This field, too, rose to the horizon, against which the old-fashioned scarecrow was clearly outlined.

Linus smiled to himself. The scarecrow was like the Gloucesters—a picturesque anachronism from which Tom Brigsteer refused to be parted. He erected one every year in whichever field he was growing cereals. Each year the scarecrow was bizarrely dressed. One year it had worn a nightshirt and a red nightcap; this year it appeared to be in full evening dress. Tom insisted that it was as efficient a way as any of deterring the pigeons that plundered the crops but it didn't look as if this one was doing his job very well. Linus narrowed his eyes. The scarecrow was some way off, but although the sun shone on it, it was quite difficult to make out very much detail. Far from scaring birds, it appeared to have attracted them. They were perched along the outstretched black-clothed arms and there seemed to be at least two on the head. Rooks, so far as Linus could judge, though he thought he caught the flash of white that indicated a magpie. Whatever they were, they weren't scared. It would be something to tease Tom about.

Or maybe not, Linus thought, switching on the ignition. It was likely Tom would be in no mood for teasing, however good-natured or well-intentioned. He put the car into gear and pulled away.

The yard was as clean as any farmyard is ever likely to be and a good bit cleaner than most. Linus put his head over the open half-door of a loose-box and studied the object of his visit. He banged his head against the door and the cow threw up her rich red head and rolled her eyes so that the whites showed. A more normal reaction would have been a look of placid amazement at such a pointless action.

Tom had seen to it that she had thick straw so that she was less likely to slip but, if she did, any fall would be cushioned. Her hooves were therefore largely hidden but he could see that the fetlocks on the hind leg were now knuckling over in the characteristically unco-ordinated way associated with BSE. He hadn't seriously doubted his initial diagnosis and there was at least a professional satisfaction in seeing it confirmed.

'Don't suppose you've changed your mind,' a voice said behind him.

Linus turned. 'Sorry, Tom. Wish I could. I'd say she's worse, wouldn't you?'

The farmer nodded. 'Going down quite quickly. Where do you want her? In or out?'

'Out. We'll have to get her in the crush to give her the Rompon. That'll bring her down. Any problem getting her across there?'

'Shouldn't be.' Tom Brigsteer nodded to his cowman who had joined them by now and opened the rest of the door. The cow came out quietly enough and was shepherded across the yard to the crush, the narrow pen as wide and as long as a cow in which it was possible to dose, drench or inject the most intransigent animal. She was unsteady on her feet and Linus knew that the stress of the crush and the injection would increase her lack of co-ordination before the muscle-relaxant did its work.

He filled his syringe while the two men penned the cow safely.

Tom Brigsteer eyed it suspiciously. 'How much are you giving her, for God's sake?' he asked.

'Twenty mil,' Linus told him. 'Yes, I know one mil is usually enough to bring a cow down but BSE has a funny effect on the brain. In fact, my own personal diagnosis would be the need for a massive dose of the stuff.' He rammed the needle into the cow's rump and slowly released the drug into the muscle. 'OK. Let her out,' he said when he had finished.

She came out unsteadily and stood uncertainly in the yard. Tom Brigsteer rubbed her head between the horns. 'How long before they come for her?'

Linus looked at his watch. 'About an hour from now. They've another one to pick up at the other end of the county first.' The cow staggered over to the narrow entrance to the yard and Linus went in after her to turn her. 'Come on, old girl, we don't want you going down where you'll do yourself an injury, now do we?'

The stockman came forward with a halter so that when the Rompon finally won, there would be no risk of her head being trapped beneath her heavy body. All the Uppertop cattle were used to being halter-led. It made handling at times like this much easier.

While he waited for the cow to go down, Linus prepared the Lethobarb solution. Killing BSE suspects posed a problem. Diagnosis was by histological examination of the brain. That meant a free bullet, which would destroy the brain, was out of the question and, since no one yet knew to what extent the disease was transmissible to man, a captive bolt was considered to pose an unacceptable risk to the operator because of the possibility of a sort of aerosol-backlash effect. The possibility was remote, but if any tissue was infective it would be brain tissue and this was a disease with too many unanswered questions. Suspects were therefore destroyed with barbiturates which was a less straightforward process than it might seem because they were still only made in the strength needed to kill dogs.

Quite suddenly the cow's unsteadiness increased and she crumbled on her side and lay, totally relaxed, while the stockman removed the halter. Linus handed him the flask of Lethobarb with its attached tube and knelt over the beast, seeking its jugular vein with his surgically-gloved hand. With the needle in the vein and the tube attached, there was nothing more to do except hold the flask aloft until its contents had emptied into the vein. It was a painless death but not a quick one and it plainly upset Tom Brigsteer.

He shook his head. 'Poor old girl,' he said. 'You didn't ought to die like this.'

Linus didn't like it much, either, but it was the only humane way which would also leave the brain intact for the Ministry's experts to examine. He decided to draw the farmer's attention to something else.

'That's a very grand scarecrow you've got this year. It looks like full evening dress.'

Tom smiled briefly. 'Aye. Meg came across the outfit at a jumble sale. He's even more impressive close up. Know what was the most difficult thing?' Linus shook his head. 'Finding a pair of white gloves. No one wears them any more.'

'Pity he's not having more effect,' Linus said. 'The birds are just sitting on him. Rooks mostly, I think. I don't think I've ever seen them quite so brazen about it before.'

Tom Brigsteer frowned. 'Still there, are they? Funny, that. They were there yesterday, and the day before. I meant to go and have a look only this business was more urgent. I wonder what the attraction is? We made him the same way we always does.'

The cowman interrupted. 'She's gone, I reckon.'

The stethoscope confirmed his opinion. Linus put his equipment back in its bucket. 'Keep the others away from her,' he said. 'Once she's gone, hose it down. Get rid of all the blood and disinfect it. A solution of one in five. Then hose that down before the rest of the herd risks burning their feet on it.'

'When will we know?'

'Three months, I'm afraid. The brain has to

be steeped in formalin for six weeks before they can start work on it. After that, the delay's due to the huge increase in reported cases. It's pretty well nationwide now.'

'Fat consolation that is,' Tom Brigsteer said bitterly. 'I just hope there aren't any more in this herd.'

'So do I,' Linus said truthfully, though in no very great expectation that it would prove to be the case. Too many of the Uppertop cows—particularly in the commercial herd—were of the crucial age, three—four—five years old, and they'd all been fed the same way as calves. Tom would be lucky indeed if he only had the one case. 'Get in touch with us immediately if you do, though, won't you? You know the symptoms now, so you'll probably identify it more quickly—if there is a next time,' he added.

He pulled in to write up his diary at roughly the same spot that he had stopped at before. Experience had taught him that if he didn't jot down his times of arrival and departure immediately, together with his mileage, he quite simply wouldn't remember these details so beloved of civil servants in Whitehall who knew as much about the ins and outs of veterinary work as he knew about nuclear physics. As it was, his diaries tended to reveal a fair degree of artistic licence, though never as to where he'd been and what he'd done. It was only the times that he occasionally took liberties with, simply because he had forgotten to note either his time of departure from one place or when he arrived at the next. Or both. He slipped the notebook back into the glove compartment and looked at the pasture. It was a satisfying field, complete with a mature oak to one side that spread its convoluted limbs over the grazing. All it needed to present the perfect picture of an English landscape was a group of mares and foals. With that addition it would have been pure Stubbs. It was Stubbs, not Constable, who captured the true essence of the English landscape, Linus thought, and he did so because it was never his prime purpose.

Linus reached over to the ignition and his eyes drifted up towards Tom Brigsteer's rather splendid scarecrow. The birds were still there. It really was very odd, especially in a field of cereals. He would have expected them to be mainly pigeons, with perhaps the odd pheasant among them, but they still looked like rooks and they'd apparently been there for days.

He didn't like unsolved puzzles. He glanced at his watch. There was time enough to go and investigate. He ought to get Tom's permission, of course, but in the circumstances perhaps it might be more tactful not to. He knew him well enough to be reasonably sure no offence would be taken and it would be a simple enough matter to walk straight up the tram-lines left by spraying tractors. He locked the car and climbed the gate.

He realized as he drew near that the scarecrow had its back to him and that the approach of a total stranger was not discomposing the birds. They saw him—watched him, even—but made no attempt to fly even the few yards to the trees bordering the field. Others were too engrossed even to look up. He drew level with it and then made his way through the crop taking care to do as little damage as possible.

The first thing to hit him, which it did with a sudden shift of the summer breeze, was the smell. Linus was a vet and perfectly familiar with the smell of putrefaction. It was not a smell one associated with straw-filled scarecrows. He made his way round to the front and for the first time the rooks showed signs of unease, the more apprehensive of them lifting off and circling.

Linus looked at the scarecrow and his stomach heaved. He had had regrets, but no qualms, about putting down Tom's cow, and if the Ministry had required it, he would have been perfectly willing to sever the head himself. But a cow was a cow. Humans were different and Tom Brigsteer's scarecrow was nothing if not human—or had been. The head lolled to one side and the eyes had gone, along with most of the flesh on the face. Rooks were efficient scavengers. There were signs that the birds had started to peck through the black tail-coat and the white shirt-front. Linus put out an unwilling hand and touched the arm. He felt flesh under the sleeve. His stomach heaved again and he turned away to vomit. That was when he noticed a grey horsehair wig—a judge's wig—on the ground beside the figure. It didn't look as if it had been carefully placed there but more as if it had fallen, perhaps dislodged by the carrion-seekers. Pinned quite firmly to it was a small square of black material. Wasn't that all that the notorious black cap consisted of, in the days when hanging was still legal? Rigor mortis had long since worn off and the figure was kept upright by two broomsticks, one vertically up a trouser-leg and out at the neck, the other through the sleeves. Whoever had put this thing here had even gone to the trouble of giving it the white gloves Tom had mentioned. Linus glanced around. Of the original occupant of the clothes, there was no sign.

Linus returned to his car several knots faster than he had climbed the hill and not only because the incline was in his favour. Nor was he so diligent in his respect for the crop.

The cow was still in the yard when Linus got back to the farm and Tom was clearly surprised to see him.

'Forgotten a form, have we?' he said when he

saw who it was.

'Nothing so simple,' Linus told him. 'That scarecrow of yours. I suppose you did make it in the traditional way?'

''Course I did. We always does. Why, what's wrong?' He looked at Linus suspiciously and suspicion changed to concern. 'Whatever's the matter? You looks like you'd seen something quite nasty in the woodshed.'

'Not so much the woodshed as your field of oats,' Linus told him. 'I think you'd better call the police.'

* * *

Detective-Inspector Netley was a sharp young man, younger than Linus had expected and certainly young enough to have delusions of intellectual grandeur. His manner suggested that he regarded the more bucolic occupations—among which he clearly included veterinary science—as the province of the mildly retarded. Linus suspected that his accompanying detective-sergeant must have been something of a trial to him since his stolid appearance and pronounced Oxfordshire accent were a clear indication of his rural origins. Linus did not fall into the trap of assuming that a man who spoke little, necessarily thought little and he rather suspected that when the detective-sergeant had something to say, it might well be worth listening to.

They tramped across the fields from the farm, approaching the scarecrow from the direction opposite to that which Linus had previously used and stood briefly in a silent semi-circle round the figure. Then Netley stepped forward and studied it more closely.

'You're right, Mr Rintoul,' he said at last, in a tone which indicated surprise that his diagnosis and Linus's would coincide. 'He's dead.'

Linus felt irritated. A five-year-old would have realized that. He bit back the sarcastic comment he would have loved to utter and smiled instead. 'I'm so glad you agree,' he murmured.

The detective-sergeant glanced sharply at him, as if he suspected an underlying meaning behind the innocuous words but wasn't sure whether Linus was capable of irony. 'And from which direction did you come, sir?' he asked.

Linus indicated the tractor-lines and the detective-sergeant took himself off unbidden to have a closer look.

'Your boots, sir,' he said when he returned and Linus, correctly interpreting this as a wish to see their soles, obediently turned up his foot. The policeman nodded. 'That's the ones. No other footprints between here and there, sir, and they look very fresh.'

Netley was gazing up at the trees edging the

field. The branches of two dead elms were heavy with rooks and more perched on the fence-rails. He nodded acknowledgement of his assistant's observation. 'Are those the birds you mentioned, Mr Rintoul?' he asked.

Linus studied them. 'They're rooks, certainly,' he said, punctiliously accurate. 'Whether they're the same rooks, I can't say. I'm afraid one rook looks very like another to me.'

The inspector, to whom Linus suspected a bird was a bird, made no immediate comment. 'But you think it likely,' he said at last, after further scrutiny of their observers.

'Highly probable. After all, they're not going to stray far from their dinner, are they?'

Netley declined to be drawn and his attention returned to some of the more curious aspects of the corpse's situation. 'I don't suppose either of you gentlemen knows who this is?' he asked.

Both Linus and Tom Brigsteer pleaded ignorance and Linus forbore to point out that it would have been difficult to recognize any face in that condition.

The senior policeman straightened up. 'Can't do any more now until Forensic have had a look. You'll have to stay till they get here,' he told his sergeant. His glance drifted to the trees again. 'Wish they wouldn't sit there watching us,' he said. 'I know they're only birds, but it's unnerving.'

His sergeant followed his gaze. 'Ah well, it would be,' he said stolidly. 'They're the messengers of the dark, you see.' He offered no clarification of his statement and seemed unaware of the suspicious glance his superior threw him.

Linus smiled to himself. Netley thinks the mickey's being taken, he thought. He's wrong. Whatever the man means, he's perfectly serious. Aloud, he said, 'Have you two been working together long?'

Netley started back towards the farm. 'Not long,' he said. 'I've only just been shifted here. Something over three weeks, I'd say. I've been with an urban force so they decided I'd better have a sergeant who knew the country and its ways. I dare say they were right.'

'I don't know about you, Tom,' Linus said when Netley was monopolizing the farm telephone, 'but I could do with a good stiff drink after this. The pub ought to be open by now. What say you?'

Tom cast a dour look at the back of Netley's neck. 'Good idea. I'll just let Bill know where we are. Shan't be sorry to be off the premises when they come to take the old girl away, anyway.'

They left Netley to it and took Linus's car to the Red Lion. It was one of those pubs that had been tarted up to confirm to the townsman's idea of a country pub, with machine-stamped brasses and Alken prints, and a brass peacock in the fireplace, its outspread tail disguising an empty fireplace that needed no disguise. All the same, the beer was good and the bar meals better.

'Fancy some lunch?' Linus asked.

Tom shook his head. 'Gone off me food a bit today. Can't think why.'

Upon reflection, Linus—who had been feeling quite hungry—decided that he had, too, and they contented themselves with a pint each of the pub's own home-brew. By tacit mutual consent, they both avoided referring to the more gruesome of the morning's events, and not because of listening ears. In fact, the bar was almost empty, the only occupant being a young woman. Young, that is, Linus amended, by comparison with himself. She was perhaps in her mid-thirties with dark hair and a pleasant face that was attractive without being particularly striking. It looked a good-humoured sort of face. She dressed quietly but well and entirely appropriately for a would-be up-market country pub. He glanced down at floor level. Her shoes were sensible, as befitted a countrywoman, but they had sufficient heel to show her ankles to advantage, and Linus was very definitely an ankles man. Hers were good. It took him ten seconds to absorb that much before Tom claimed his attention.

'So what are the odds on my getting another

case?' he was asking.

'Given the balance of your herd and the product you've been rearing calves on, I have to say you'll be lucky if that's the only one,' Linus said, unwilling to add to the man's depression but equally unwilling to raise false hopes. 'Let's hope that's the only case to strike your Gloucesters.'

'Amen to that,' Tom Brigsteer said with feeling and raised his glass to confirm the prayer. 'How many cases get to market before the symptoms are too noticeable?'

'Quite a few but usually they become noticeable in the stress conditions of the saleyard. We've picked a few up there.'

Tom nodded. 'Aye, you would.'

A brief silence ensued and Linus was aware that the young woman had left her seat and was hovering quite close to them. He turned and smiled. The inclusion of a third person in the conversation, particularly a stranger, would keep it general and that might be no bad thing. ''Morning,' he said and then glanced at the clock behind the bar. 'Good afternoon might be more accurate. Don't think I've seen you here before.' He knew perfectly well he hadn't, partly because he would have remembered those ankles and partly because he hardly ever came in here.

'No, it's my first visit. I'm new to the area,' she said and hesitated as if reluctant to broach what was on her mind. 'I couldn't help overhearing some of your conversation,' she went on finally. 'Are you by any chance a vet?' The question could have meant either of them but was clearly directed at Linus.

'Yes,' Linus said cautiously, no more smitten than any doctor or lawyer at the prospect of a drink being interrupted by a total stranger seeking free professional advice. 'I'm a Ministry vet, though. Not in general practice.'

'But you must know vets who are—well enough to recommend one, I mean.'

Linus's caution increased. When it became a matter of recommendations, professional ethics strewed the path with tin-tacks. 'What seems to be the problem?' he asked with the sinking feeling that it was a question he might well regret.

'I've only just moved here from the London area,' she explained. 'I breed dogs in a small way. I don't suppose you know them—Amazonian Vampire Dogs?' Linus was obliged to admit to total ignorance while privately thinking they sounded rather unpleasant. 'No,' she went on, 'I thought you wouldn't: they're very rare indeed. I lived in Mexico for a while and that's where I came across them, so when I came back to Britain, my dogs naturally came too. I've been in Oxfordshire for two or three months now and, with so much to do, I hadn't got around to finding a good vet. Now I'm a bit worried: the dogs have been off-colour for some days. Nothing specific that I can point to and say this is wrong or that's not right. Just a sort of all-round under-the-weatherness and I really should get them looked at.'

Linus was about to agree that it would be a good idea when Tom butted in.

'Whereabouts are you living, then?' he asked. 'Can't say as I've seen you about before.'

'Not in this village,' she told him. 'Long Blessington—just up the road.'

Tom nodded and Linus thought he detected a hint of reserve in the farmer's attitude. 'I know where Long Blessington is. Whereabouts in it are you?'

'The other end of it. Just beyond the village proper, actually. There's a dear little thatched stone cottage that stands slightly apart. It's not on the main road but you can see it from there. It's just up a little lane and near the duck-pond.'

'I know it.' Tom returned to his pint as if his interest in the subject died with the answer. Linus was puzzled. Tom Brigsteer could be as uncommunicative as any other countryman when it suited him but he could also be loquacious to the point of garrulity. He had told Linus once that Brigsteers had farmed in this part of the county for four hundred years and Linus knew his memory went back over several generations. He had no doubt at all that, had he wanted to, Tom could have given the woman a potted history of her cottage and its previous inhabitants that would go back a hundred years and quite possibly more. It was the sort of information he enjoyed imparting even though it tended to bore the pants off those listeners who were not intimately connected with the place under scrutiny. For some reason this occasion was different and Linus was intrigued.

'Have you thought of asking another dog-person in the area which practice they use?' he suggested. Pet-owners could be seduced by a good bedside manner. Dog-breeders were harder to con: they wanted good results and small bills and protested with their feet if they weren't forthcoming. The recommendation from a breeder of a vet they had been using for years was worth far more than even the recommendation of another vet.

She hesitated. 'I've thought of that and I know it sounds silly, but I'd rather not. One of the reasons I moved to Long Blessington—apart from the fact that the cottage was cheaper than I'd expected to have to pay—was that there's quite a little enclave of AVDs there and I thought it would be . . . well, chummy. Only it hasn't worked out quite like that and, to be quite honest, I'd rather none of them knew I was having any bother.'

Linus glanced at Tom, who could probably have enlightened her as to the reason for her cottage's low price and followed it up with a character assessment of the people to whom she was referring, but Tom was engrossed in his ale and said nothing.

'I'll tell you what,' Linus suggested. 'You invite me back for a cup of coffee and then, naturally, I'll see your dogs and if you happen to mention there's something not quite right, I could volunteer to have a quick look—just to advise you whether you really do need to get your own vet on to it, of course. How does that strike you?'

Her face lit up and changed from merely attractive to a combination of radiant, relieved and mischievous. It was a combination Linus was pleased to have provoked. 'That would be perfect,' she said. 'Tell me, Mr . . . ?' Her voice tailed off inquiringly.

'Rintoul. Linus Rintoul.'

'Helen Glenbarr. Tell me, Mr Rintoul, could I interest you in a cup of coffee?'

'Easily, though I'd prefer us to drop the formality. Tom, any objections if I leave you to it?'

Tom Brigsteer looked at Linus and then at Helen and then at Linus again. He shrugged. 'No skin off my nose. I've plenty to do. It's your life you're messing with.' He drained his glass and slapped Linus on the shoulder. 'Don't get me wrong, matey, but I hopes I don't see you again for a long, long time. Not professionally, anyway.'

* * *

Helen's cottage was certainly small. There were two rooms downstairs with a kitchen added on and, Linus assumed, there would be two bedrooms upstairs with a bathroom over the kitchen. The garden was not huge but it was disproportionately large in a village where every available decent-sized garden had been divided up to provide nice, expensive building plots for outsiders. Linus frowned. Picturesque cottages, however small, with large gardens were usually at a premium. He wondered why this one had been relatively cheap. Probably the drains, he thought, and dismissed it.

The Amazonian Vampire Dogs fitted the scale of the house to perfection. Linus had had only the very haziest idea of what to expect and was quite mistaken. His immediate reaction when he was shown into the sitting-room and the dogs rushed in to greet him was to stand stock still for fear of trampling on them.

'Puppies, I suppose,' he commented.

Helen laughed. 'No, those are adults.' She picked one up and held it out to him.

Linus took it gingerly. It was about the size of a half-grown Chihuahua but its profuse coat turned it into a ball of fluff. It was red and white and its high-set, tightly curled tail, pointed black nose and tiny pricked ears indicated that it was some kind of spitz breed. Standing still, the dogs looked like pompoms with a smaller pompom for a head. Moving, they resembled clockwork pompoms. There was a surprisingly solid body under all that fur but, even so, the bones were necessarily frail. It was no breed for a family with boisterous children.

'Not what I expected,' he commented. 'Aren't you terrified of stepping on them?'

'They're remarkably astute at knowing when to get out of the way,' Helen told him. 'All the same, I tend to pen them when I've got visitors.'

'Why the name?' Linus went on. 'It seems singularly inappropriate.'

'They like to sit on a shoulder and snuggle up to the neck,' she told him. 'It keeps them warm and, because they're so small, they don't often fall off. They're very affectionate so they keep licking the side of the neck—the jugular vein, you see. The story is that if you annoy them, or move suddenly, or if they've been bewitched, they sink their teeth into the vein and feed on the blood. An evil goddess is supposed to have given them as presents to her enemies. I doubt if there's a grain of truth in it, but it's a colourful legend.'

'Pure codswallop, I should imagine,' Linus agreed. 'And what about the Amazonian bit? Is that equally imaginative?'

'No. That's closer to the truth, though for "Amazon" it might be more accurate to read "Central America". Their remains crop up only rarely in archaeological digs but when they do, the range is fairly wide: north into southern Texas and south as far as Belize. There's one school of thought that suggests they're nothing more exotic than dwarf Chihuahuas, but we fanciers choose not to accept so prosaic an origin.'

Linus examined the little bitch he was holding. 'The head is quite different,' he said, 'though I suppose that could have been bred for over the years. As for "dwarf", well, it depends whether the word is being used colloquially, as a synonym for "small", or scientifically, in which case I think not: it would take an X-ray and expert diagnosis to be sure, but the bones feel too straight and the joints too sound to warrant calling them dwarves.'

Once the dogs had got over the excitement of a visitor, they settled down and Linus could see what Helen meant. They were, on the whole, noticeably more listless than was usual in small dogs. Their temperatures were entirely normal, the gums and mouth-linings neither flushed nor pale. Palpation revealed no apparent internal abnormalities.

'I can't find anything wrong at all,' he told their owner. 'On a clinical level, they seem entirely normal, though I have to agree with you that I'd have expected a higher level of general activity in dogs of this size. Large dogs are prone to just lie around most of the day. Small ones aren't.'

'What do you suggest?' Helen asked.

'Not a great deal, I'm afraid. A broad-spectrum antibiotic might not be a bad idea and maybe a vitamin injection. There's a vet over Enstone way who won't be offended if you tell him I've seen them and that's what I suggest, subject to his own opinion, of course—and he's far more up in small animal medicine than I am, so he might well have something better to suggest. It's not exactly on your doorstep and it's only a small practice because he owns the quarantine kennels over there, but if he'll take you on, he's good—only for God's sake don't tell anyone *I* recommended him. Say you heard it on the grapevine, or something. David Thelwall's his name.'

She smiled gratefully. 'Thank you. I'll make an appointment for as soon as I can. How about that coffee now?'

Linus grinned. 'I hoped you hadn't forgotten,' he said.

While she was in the kitchen, he looked about him. A room said a lot about its owner. Some were designed to impress the visitor. Others were furnished purely for the owner's comfort and pleasure. This was one of the others. The carpet was worn, vaguely oriental and old rather than antique; the loose covers of the sofa were of the same chintz as the curtains and the only upholstered chair was a plain green that picked up one of the colours in the chintz. The only other chair was an old Windsor rocker beside the huge open fireplace and the imprint on the seat cushion betrayed the fact that this was probably the chair Helen preferred to sit in. There was a small bookcase with a fairly eclectic selection of books: several disparate paperbacks, rather more dog-books, some show catalogues, a uniformly bound set of Dickens of the sort widely sold in the 'thirties. There was a Complete Shakespeare which had the indefinable look of not having been opened since it left the publisher, and the three essentials of any civilized home: a Bible, a dictionary and an atlas. The last two seemed the more often used. There were also one or two exhibition catalogues.

Helen Glenbarr's pictures were rather more modest in scope than those that lined Linus's own walls. Her taste—or perhaps her pocket—ran to short-run signed lithographs by contemporary painters. Linus remembered her clothes and her shoes. It probably wasn't her pocket, he decided. He looked at the pictures again. Good, but a bit bland for his taste. Still, it wasn't often one met a woman with a similar interest.

He turned as she came in with a tray. 'I've been snooping,' he said unapologetically. 'You've some nice pictures.'

'Thank you. There are more but I like to change them about. Otherwise I find I stop looking at them.'

If they were less bland, Linus thought, you wouldn't need to, but that wasn't something one could say aloud. At least she recognized the fact. 'You went to the Dali exhibition?' His head gestured briefly in the direction of the catalogue.

'And got visual indigestion,' she said. 'There wasn't one picture I'd want to live with but one can only admire his technique.'

Linus nodded. 'I enjoy looking at surrealist pictures but they're just that little bit too disturbing to want to see them every day.'

'It's a good job not everyone feels like us, I suppose,' Helen said. 'If they did, there'd have been no patrons. Do you enjoy being a Ministry vet?'

The abrupt change of topic took Linus by surprise. 'I suppose I do,' he said after a brief consideration. 'I've been doing it a long time. I used to be in general practice but the hours got my wife down.'

He wondered if it was his imagination that a veil of reserve drifted between them.

'Do you have any children?' she went on.

'Two, but they're grown up and on their own

now, of course. We divorced a long time ago,' he volunteered. 'More settled hours didn't help.'

He knew then that the veil had not been imaginary. 'I'm a widow,' she said. 'No children.'

'I'm sorry.' It was the standard response and Linus wasn't sure whether it referred to the first statement or the second, or both. What's more, it wasn't true. He was actually quite glad there was no husband.

'There's no reason why you should be,' she commented briskly. 'Neither situation is your fault.'

Such a matter-of-fact and entirely realistic response was not at all what Linus had expected and it took him aback. He changed the subject. 'Do you work?' he asked.

'I'm a lab technician,' she told him. 'I've a B.Sc. but I only work part-time so the dizzier heights aren't open to me. It leaves me more time to look after the dogs. Little ones like these need a midday meal.'

'From what you were saying before, I take it you don't think the other AVD breeders would be much help?'

'To be honest with you, they're a very odd lot. I came back to England five or six years ago and started showing the dogs—there wasn't much opportunity for that in Mexico, but over there, when they were shown, mine did well.

Over here they do very well in Variety classes—classes where there are several different breeds competing. They do less well in Breed classes and not at all well if the judge is an AVD specialist. That could mean that I'm deluding myself as to their quality, but I know I'm not: mine are as good as the top winners here and better than many of the ones that get put up over them.'

Linus knew treacherous ground when he saw it and stepped back from that particular quagmire. 'Yet you moved here,' he pointed out. 'You said something about hoping it would be more . . . "chummy", I think was your word.'

She nodded. 'I'd come from abroad with a number of dogs—there's considerable jealousy in some corners of the dog-game towards people who import one dog, let alone several. It's regarded in some quarters as the canine equivalent of a Porsche or a Rolls-Royce. Silly, really, but that's how it is. Then, of course, they didn't really know me and didn't make much effort to do so. I wanted to live in the country anyway, and I thought it might be a sensible step to come to Long Blessington. Do you know Morwenna Leyburn?'

'The name means nothing at all.'

'She's the leading light in the breed. She's a cut above most dog-breeders—socially, I mean—and she likes to surround herself with her social inferiors, provided they're suitably adoring. I'm not, I'm afraid. There's something about her that makes the hairs on the back of my neck stand on end, if you know what I mean. Quite irrational, of course, but I managed to convince myself that if I lived more or less on her doorstep, better familiarity might at least make it possible for us to get on.'

'I deduce from your tone that it didn't work.'

'That's right. If we happen to bump into each other in the village she gazes into the middle distance at a point just above my shoulder. At shows, on the other hand, she's uncharacteristically effusive. There are three other AVD people in the village and they take their line from her, though one of them did speak to me once. He asked me how long I intended to stick with a breed in which I wasn't successful.'

'What did you tell him?'

'I said I'd bought them in the first place because I thought they were delightful and I didn't see what not winning had to do with it. I also told him I knew damn well they were good because of what they'd done in their country of origin and that, sooner or later, they'd get their deserts.'

'What was his reaction to that?'

'He said I could bank on it. Only I don't think he meant it in quite the way I had.'

Linus privately thought she was right,

though it was a retort to which she had laid herself wide open. He didn't say so, however: detected a hint of desolation under the defiance which hinted at emotional quicksands into which he was not ready to be drawn. He glanced at his watch.

'Look,' he said, 'pleasant though this is, I really can't sit around all day drinking coffee and talking dogs. Why don't you put the dogs in your car and I'll guide you to Thelwall's place and introduce you to him. That way there won't be any difficulty about it.'

CHAPTER TWO

Like Linus, David Thelwall could find nothing obviously amiss but he was able to proffer one alternative suggestion.

'I don't suppose you've been putting down rat poison?' he asked.

Helen was horrified. 'Certainly not. I don't think I'd agree to it even if I had a problem with the creatures—which I haven't.'

'Your neighbours?'

'I suppose one of the farms may have laid some,' she said doubtfully, 'but these dogs couldn't have got at it—their exercise is taken almost entirely in the garden. They're not a breed that needs miles of walking every day.'

Thelwall looked at the dogs and smiled. 'No, I don't suppose they do. Don't worry about it—it was a shot in the dark, that's all. I'd expect some more positive symptoms if it was poisoning. They're appealing little things, aren't they? Are they always red and white?'

'No. They can be anything and white, preferably with quite a lot of the white: we don't much like just a few white hairs on the chest and toes. People say they all look the same but they don't, of course. There's actually quite a considerable variation in the markings.'

'No two dogs ever do look exactly the same,' Linus commented. 'Not even black Labradors, though people who haven't got them think they do.'

Linus drove back to Oxford relatively well pleased with the way the day had turned out. He had not been looking forward to putting down Tom Brigsteer's cow, and discovering a body in such macabre circumstances was definitely an experience he would be happy never to repeat, but even that had had its good side. If it hadn't been for the body, he and Tom would not have gone to the Red Lion. Experience had taught Linus not to overrate his chances with the opposite sex but it did seem as if, in Helen Glenbarr, he had met someone with whom he had enough in common to make it worthwhile to pursue the acquaintance. He would leave it for a day or two and then find a pretext for telephoning her.

* * *

A young policeman called round that evening to take a long statement. He was polite and deferential and changed Linus's ordinary phraseology into policemanese. Linus, who thought he had been driving from A to B, discovered, when his statement was read over to him, that he had in fact been proceeding in a westerly direction. He protested that he hadn't said that—hadn't even thought of it like that, but the young man was adamant.

'Is it accurate, sir?' he asked.

'Well, yes, it's *accurate*, but it's not what I said.'

'Then that's all right, sir. It's clearer, you see. Leaves no room for ambiguity.'

Linus was mystified as to how a statement that one was travelling from one named village to another could possibly be ambiguous but, a civil servant himself, he knew when bureaucracy had the upper hand, and signed the statement.

'I take it that the fact that they've sent you and it's all very civilized means I'm not under suspicion of doing away with whoever myself?' It was a joking remark designed—in so far as it had a design—to ease some of the tension inevitably caused by the necessity of detailing in cold words what he had found. Linus forgot that a sense of humour does not figure prominently among the average policeman's characteristics.

This one was no exception. He looked at Linus with deep suspicion. 'Why, sir? Would you have expected us to suspect you?'

Linus, irritated, wondered whether policemen went on special courses to teach them how to answer questions with questions. 'I imagine you must suspect everyone, at least initially,' he said testily. 'I only meant that the fact that I haven't been hauled off in a Black Maria for questioning at a police station perhaps means that someone is reasonably satisfied that my involvement began and ended with finding the body.'

The policeman who must, Linus thought bitterly, have been all of twenty-three years old, permitted himself the merest flicker of a smile. '"Black Maria",' he echoed. 'What a nice, old-fashioned word! I don't think I've ever heard it used before. But don't worry, Mr Rintoul. In a case like yours we send an ordinary police car. If we're feeling very kindly disposed, it might even be an unmarked one.' He zipped up his document case. 'Thank you for your time, Mr Rintoul. That's all I need for now.'

Linus saw him to the door. 'Do they know who the dead man was?' he asked.

The policeman fitted his hat firmly on to his head before answering. 'As to that, I couldn't say, sir. Curious about it, are you?'

'Naturally enough in the circumstances, don't you think?'

'Possibly.' The tone hinted that it was a most unnatural curiosity. 'I dare say they'll release that information to the Press—when they have it,' he added. 'Good night, Mr Rintoul.'

Linus closed the door behind him with unwonted emphasis. Young jackanapes! He had somehow succeeded in making Linus feel ninety-three and as guilty as hell and Linus knew it was his own fault for having expected a policeman to give the sort of responses a normal citizen would have made.

Two days later the young man's prognosis proved correct. The body that had been discovered at Uppertop Farm—a statement which implied a previous reference to the event, although Linus had not found one—had been identified as that of Mr Justice Wingfield, who had only recently presided over a particularly nasty trial during the course of which threats had been made against nearly everyone involved, from the judge himself to the humblest witness. The inference of this was somewhat offset by the further information that it appeared the judge had died from a heart attack. The circumstances of the body's discovery were not revealed, a matter for which

Linus felt some gratitude, though he would have been interested to see some speculation as to how the judge got himself into his extraordinary situation and whether he had done so before or after the heart-attack.

That same morning the post brought him a catalogue and an invitation to the private view of the pictures detailed inside at a gallery from which he had bought once or twice. A quick run-through suggested that there was probably nothing likely to appeal to him particularly, since turn-of-the-century genre pictures, however excellent, left him cold. Still, it had its uses. This was the pretext he needed to contact Helen Glenbarr again.

His suspicions about the pictures proved correct but there was the added bonus that Helen's comments were intelligent and relevant even though their taste did not always coincide. He had once gone to an exhibition with a woman who went into schoolgirlish raptures over anything with a cat in it, and another time had had the misfortune to take a woman who was acutely embarrassed by the presence of nudes on the wall, forbidding him—in unnecessarily carrying tones—to look at them. Helen presented no such problems and he had no urge to rush her out of the gallery or invent a suddenly remembered professional visit. He invited her to lunch instead.

He wanted to know more about her, but her

past included a dead husband and although she had previously appeared to be able to take references to him without recourse to a handkerchief, it was the sort of area where it would be all too easy to touch a nerve. 'Do you mind talking about your husband?' he asked. 'I shan't be offended if you do,' he added hastily.

Her smile reassured him. 'I don't mind at all,' she said. 'In fact, I'd quite like to. Most people avoid the subject. I think they expect me to break down and embarrass them.'

'They probably just don't know what to say,' Linus said. 'It's the sort of question that can very easily look like morbid curiosity. What did he do?'

'He was an engineer. That's what took us to Mexico. He was working on an irrigation project—quite a sophisticated one: not just a collection of little drainage ditches. We'd been there about two years and loved it to start with. The work was just the sort of thing Peter had always wanted to do. He felt he was doing something that was of practical help to a very poor population and, in addition to that, we both loved the people. But then it began to go sour.' She stopped, clearly unhappy.

'You don't have to tell me if you don't want to,' Linus assured her.

She shook her head. 'I know I don't and it's not something I've talked about before, but I'd like to now, if you don't mind. Do you?'

'It's up to you. I shan't be offended if you decide to stop now and I don't suppose I shall be embarrassed if you go on.'

Helen smiled briefly. 'I don't know if anyone's ever told you before, but you're a good man, Linus Rintoul.' She took a deep breath before plunging into the rest of her story. 'He discovered that the purpose of the irrigation wasn't quite what he had thought it to be. It wasn't to grow wheat or rice or beans or whatever, but to establish acres and acres of marijuana up in the mountains for sale over the border in the US.'

'Is it legal in Mexico?'

'No, of course not. Why?'

'"Acres and acres" would be easily identifiable from the air. Surely the police would act?'

'Not if the right policemen were paid enough money. Mexico works like that, I'm afraid. Anyway, Peter worried and worried over it and then, because there was another Englishman involved, he went to the Consul, who advised him who was the safest person to talk to. We both hoped it would all be cleared up quickly and then maybe the government would take over the project and direct it as Peter had originally expected it to be directed—to food production. We'd agreed that if that happened, he'd offer to stay on at a reduced salary to complete the job, only it didn't quite work out like that. I've never been quite sure what happened and I suspect no one really knows but there was some sort of accident with a sluice gate which should have been closed, and he drowned. The water must have come in a tremendous rush because he was a very strong swimmer.'

'What happened to the other Englishman?'

'He's in jail for a very long time—and Mexican jails aren't very nice places, by all accounts. It was a bit unfair, really, because none of the Mexicans involved—and with far more responsibility for what was going on than Matthew Kirkstall—even got as far as the courts.'

'So then you came back to England?'

'Not immediately, no. I told you we loved it there. For a long time it seemed to me that I ought to stay in the place we'd become so attached to, but after a while I began to realize that the real reason I was staying on was because I couldn't bear to tear myself away from Peter's memory. It was almost as if I believed that if I stayed there long enough, he'd come back. In the end I spoke to a priest about it and he said it was a common enough phenomenon and if I let it take hold, it would stunt the rest of my life. I hated him for saying that but when I'd had a few days to calm down and think about it, I began to suspect that he might be right and after a few more months of pretending he wasn't, I gave up and admitted that he was. That's when I decided to come home, get myself a job, and start again.'

'Have you regretted it?'

'No. It hasn't worked out quite as I expected, perhaps: I always feel very much on the edge of things. I suppose that's partly why I was so keen to get myself accepted with the Amazonian Vampire people. Still, as my father used to say, if the rope breaks, tie a knot and go on.'

'A good naval expression,' Linus commented. 'Was that your father's profession?'

'You're very astute,' she exclaimed with an inflection that wasn't entirely complimentary.

'Not really. Just Bristol-born and bred,' he said modestly. 'Not Navy, exactly, but the ships didn't differ very much—not when that expression was coined, anyway.'

'He was a naval man, as a matter of fact,' she said in a milder tone and then hesitated before continuing. 'Have you ever been to a dog show?'

'A couple of times,' Linus admitted cautiously. 'I went to Crufts once and to a show just before Christmas at the NEC [*Dead Spit*].'

She nodded. 'That would be the LKA. Did you enjoy them?'

'Not especially.' Linus thought the understatement covered it rather well.

Her face fell. 'Pity. I was going to ask you if

you'd like to come to one with me. Outdoor summer shows are quite different from the winter indoor ones,' she added hopefully.

Linus thought about it quickly. He hadn't the slightest desire to go to another dog show as long as he lived, but he liked Helen Glenbarr and she must feel similarly about him to have extended the invitation in the first place. He always felt rather diffident in his relationships with women, largely because they hadn't been crowned with success in the past. An opportunity to extend the acquaintance was not to be rejected lightly, particularly when it had emanated from her.

'As long as it's a weekend I don't mind having the opportunity of revising my opinion,' he said.

'Next Sunday—and it's not very far. Windsor. It has the reputation of never having bad weather and the castle makes a superlative backdrop.'

'Do you stand a chance of doing well?'

She grimaced. 'I did, but it's a complete gamble now. The judge it was supposed to be did my dogs rather well on previous occasions but he died recently and it hasn't yet been announced who's to replace him. Whoever it is, they're unlikely to go quite so strongly for my type. It will either be someone who hasn't a clue and puts up a complete mish-mash or someone who plays safe and goes for the well-known faces on the other end of the lead.'

'That's not very fair,' Linus commented, shocked as much by her apparent acceptance of the situation as by the situation itself.

'Maybe not but it happens all the time, especially with a rare breed, and I suppose in a way it's just human nature: if you're unsure, go for the faces that are reputed to have good stock. I'd rather that than lose because the judge has had a phone call telling him the shortcomings of my dogs.'

Now Linus was really shocked. 'Do people do that?'

'Some people, not many, and if it's done crudely I think most judges tell them where to get off, but if it's done subtly and in the course of a conversation to which it seems incidental, then I think a lot of judges don't realize how they're being influenced. Some of them aren't very bright.'

'If your view of the game is as cynical as that, why go on?'

'I like the dogs,' she said simply. 'I could just keep them as pets, of course, but I enjoy having puppies and in a breed like this, the only way to sell the ones you don't want to keep is to be seen at shows—preferably winning.'

'I suppose that makes sense,' Linus said doubtfully. 'It still sounds like a dodgy sport.'

'It can work both ways. I told you I'm a lab technician? I didn't tell you I work in a forensic lab. I did some of the work in a recent, rather unpleasant case and because there was a question about the efficiency with which the actual tests were done, I had to give evidence. The presiding judge was Mr Justice Wingfield, and he would have been the man to judge us on Sunday. I can't imagine seeing me in the ring would have had any influence on his placings. In fact, he must see so many witnesses that I doubt very much if he would even have recognized me in that very different context, but if I'd won, you can imagine what would have been said.'

'Mr Justice Wingfield? Wasn't that the man who had a heart attack recently?' Linus had an irrational hope that there might be two Mr Justice Wingfields. He didn't like coincidences.

'That's right. A farmer found him in one of his fields, or something. "Near Chipping Norton", they said.'

It was as accurate a statement as any, Linus supposed, and wondered whether perhaps he ought to say, 'Well, as a matter of fact . . .' but he decided against it. He had no wish to re-live his discovery through long explanations. Instead, he said, 'How odd—someone who judges dogs as well as people.'

'He wasn't unique. There are two others, I believe.'

'Wasn't that the terrorist trial where there were supposed to be all sorts of threats made against the participants?'

'That's right—but I don't think the sort of people who make threats like that are thinking of heart attacks, do you?'

Linus considered certain aspects of the Judge's fate and was glad he hadn't mentioned the details. 'Did you get any threats?' he asked.

'Just a phone call. It was a bit upsetting at the time.' She paused. 'Very upsetting, as a matter of fact. I told the police, of course, and they were very good, but there weren't any more and I gave my evidence and that was that. There's been nothing since. I was only doing my job, after all, and I expect they realized that.'

So was Mr Justice Wingfield, Linus thought, but kept it to himself. Perhaps it would do no harm to keep an eye on Helen Glenbarr. It would certainly be no penance. 'What time do you want me to put in an appearance on Sunday?' he asked instead.

* * *

The tradition of fine weather for Windsor held true and since Oxford was more or less on Helen's way to Windsor, it was she who put in an appearance at an uncomfortably early hour on Sunday. Linus did not like being driven and excused himself privately from any suspicion of chauvinism by telling himself that it didn't matter what sex the driver was. He knew, however, that this was not entirely true and that his unease was greater when the chauffeur was a woman. He therefore slid into the seat beside Helen with some reservations and then found that these were steadily eroded as she handled the car, the Oxford streets and the by-pass with the assurance of custom. There was very little traffic so early on a Sunday morning, but by the time they reached their destination it had increased without a corresponding diminution in his opinion of her capabilities.

Linus's previous brief acquaintance with dog shows had prepared him for the army of large ladies of what was usually referred to as uncertain age, towing behind them trolleys laden with dog-filled cages, blankets, towels, bags of grooming kit, collapsible chairs and, he assumed, packed lunches. Voluminous floral prints were more in evidence than the winter's tweeds but some still sported the shapeless cloth hats—in denim rather than waterproofs—that would have looked more at home in a trout stream.

Being a part of all this—helping Helen with her own trolley and cages—changed his perspective somewhat, but even so, when they reached the Amazonian Vampire Dog benches, he was forced to the conclusion that AVD fanciers were an even stranger bunch than most of the other exhibitors.

It wasn't simply that they were for the most

part well over fifty: that was to be expected with a small breed that by definition needed little formal exercise. It was their inescapable weirdness. There was one woman, younger than most, who was quite clearly dressed to fit the second word of the breed's name. She wore a very mannish black tailsuit, though the effect was somewhat spoilt by the accompaniment of a soft shirt. Her hair was improbably raven-black and drawn severely back from her face, like a ballerina's, while her face itself had been powdered almost white. Not, Linus thought dispassionately, a candidate for skin cancer. Most of those he classified as weirdos wore flowing robes and hair to match, with huge, dangling ear-rings and necklaces of chunky, home-made pottery beads. They looked like refugees from the hippy era of quarter of a century earlier—until one looked more closely at their faces, which had a sharp, discontented quality far removed from the underlying principles of flower power which Linus vaguely recalled.

One woman was indubitably the queen bee round whom the workers swarmed. She had a round, plump face which was deceptively youthful from a reasonable distance. This illusion was enhanced by her hair which was expensively blonde and cut in the severe lines of an Egyptian tomb-painting, framing the baby-face with its wide blue eyes with such precision that it might almost have been a wig. As she came closer, her real age—which Linus guessed to be in excess of sixty, though he admitted that estimating women's ages accurately was not one of his more notable skills—became apparent. She was a classic demonstration of the fact that there comes a time when the hair and skin no longer fit together, and Linus wondered why no one ever tells such women that the time has come to stroll gracefully into old age. Hearing her snap the head off a passer-by who protested about the cluttered gangway, Linus supposed that in her case, no one had ever dared. She, too, wore robes but hers were less rent-a-tenty than the others. They were dramatically purple with gold braid some two inches wide round the neck, wrists and hem and on either side of the front fastening. It might not have looked too out-of-place at a fairly normal party. At a dog show it looked bizarre, though, to do her credit, she carried it off with sufficient aplomb to make the others look underdressed. Large gold five-pointed stars hung from her ears and round her neck on the end of a heavy gold chain hung a large gold ankh which rested on her ample bosom and when she leant over her dogs, swung into whichever part of their anatomy was nearest.

Linus was not surprised when his query to Helen elicited the information that this was

Morwenna Leyburn. By comparison, Helen herself was quite idiosyncratically normal.

Ms Leyburn—Linus could see no wedding-ring yet she did not somehow seem to be a Miss—cast several sharply inquiring glances in his direction. Whether she was expecting an introduction to be made, Linus had no idea, but when none was forthcoming, she remedied the deficiency herself and came over with a bright, social smile.

'You're with Helen,' she said. 'We haven't met but if you're going to come to shows with her we shall, frequently. I'm Morwenna Leyburn.'

It was said in a manner which conveyed not simply the basic information of the words themselves, but a pronounced hint of patronage; an assumption not only that he would have heard of her, but also that he would—rightly—feel honoured to have been greeted by her almost as an equal. It was not an approach calculated to appeal to Linus even if he hadn't already had a brief character-sketch of her from Helen. He looked at her quite blankly. 'Morwenna . . .' He paused quite deliberately. '. . . Leyburn, did you say? Should I know you?'

The blue eyes, which he would never have described as warm, grew positively glacial and narrowed while she tried to determine whether he was rude or just stupid. The smile became effusive. 'There's no reason why you *should*,' she said winsomely, 'but I do hope you *will*. Have you known Helen long?'

Linus favoured her with a vague smile. 'These things are relative, don't you think? Sometimes it feels as if I met her yesterday, sometimes as if I've known her for a decade. Mind you, I always find women are like that, so it doesn't mean much, does it?'

Morwenna was no wiser about the length of their acquaintance yet could hardly press a matter which was so definitely none of her business, no matter how badly she wanted to know the answer. Nor was she any further forward in her character assessment. Stupidity seemed to be leading the field but she had a sneaking suspicion the reverse might be true. She did notice that her own introduction had not been followed by its expected reciprocation, but she was more than equal to that omission.

'And you are . . . ?' she asked.

'Rintoul,' he told her. '*Mr* Rintoul.' He despised himself for the blatant vulgarity of his reply but he had a deep-seated instinct that this was a woman accustomed to winkling out of people any information she wanted and that was closely followed by an instinct to tell her as little as possible. Helen had said that Morwenna Leyburn made the hairs on her neck stand on end. Linus wouldn't have put it quite like that, but he knew exactly what she meant.

'And is this your first dog show, *Mr* Rintoul?' she inquired, laying undue stress on the title.

Linus managed a convincingly amazed smile. 'Good lord, no,' he said.

'I don't think I've seen you about before.' It was a disbelieving statement.

'Probably not.' Linus was clearly unperturbed by that fact. 'This isn't my breed and we're usually on a different day.' He was quite proud of being able to use a phraseology that marked him out as an aficionado. 'I don't go to all that many shows,' he added to clinch the matter. 'Pressure of work, you know.'

'And what is your breed?' she persisted.

'Bull Terriers,' he equivocated. He only had one and it was an American Pit Bull which was not eligible for Kennel Club registration and therefore couldn't be shown. 'I also had a brief association with Antiguan Truffle Dogs.' That, at least, was true.

She seemed satisfied, but puzzled, and Linus had a shrewd suspicion that when she got home she would check him out in the pages of past catalogues.

Any further conversation was thwarted by a hearty, 'Good God, it's Rintoul!' Linus turned to discover his saviour was John Chilson, a vet with whom he had been at college and with whom he had had a sporadic acquaintance in recent years. Linus had no idea whether Chilson was known to Morwenna Leyburn, though he did not appear to know her, but he saw her eyes go straight to the newcomer's tie whose stripes announced his Kennel Club membership, and he had the impression that she was rapidly revising her assessment of Mr Rintoul.

Chilson looked at the benches. 'Shouldn't have thought this was your sort of breed,' he said.

'It's not,' Linus told him. He stretched out an arm towards Helen to draw her into the conversation. 'Do you know Helen Glenbarr?' he asked. 'I'm being her dog's body for the day. Helen, John Chilson and I were at college together.' He cursed himself as soon as the words were out. The Leyburn woman was ostensibly attending to her dogs and although she had her back to them, Linus could almost feel the draught from her flapping ears. If she knew who—or rather, what—Chilson was, she would also know that Linus was a vet. It was hardly a secret, of course, but she was just someone from whom his instinct was to conceal as much as possible.

Chilson looked at her appreciatively. 'Not a bad way to spend a free day,' he commented. 'Why don't the two of you come and have a drink?'

'You go,' Helen told Linus. 'I like to stay with the dogs until we've been in the ring.'

Linus shook his head. 'It's a bit too early for

me,' he told Chilson. 'Maybe later.'

Chilson glanced at Helen again and smiled as if he suspected that 'too early' was just the excuse. 'After the breed judging, then. If I'm not in the Secretary's office, get them to page me. OK?'

Linus promised and when Chilson had gone, Helen said, 'You could have gone, you know. You don't have to stay.'

'I know, but it really is too early. I was only partly being gallant. Besides, I don't want to miss the judging and one drink with one of the Chilsons of this world has a habit of turning into two or three.'

As the morning wore on, the day became oppressive and the dogs restless as if in anticipation of a storm. People unfastened the canvas sides of the benching tent to let more air circulate, an action Linus thought they might well regret if a storm broke with the force such sultriness betokened.

It was getting on for one o'clock before Vampire Dogs were called to the ring and Linus was more than a little interested to see who had taken the place of the dead judge. One look at the replacement was enough to tell Linus that he had more in common with Morwenna than with Helen. A tall man in his early thirties, he had the gaunt look of the ascetic accentuated by a rather thin beard and long, lank hair tied back in a pony-tail. Looking at him, Linus unconsciously fingered with some satisfaction his own neatly-trimmed but gratifyingly thick beard. Like Morwenna, the man affected a long robe, though his was in dull crimson with braid to match. The effect was to enhance the ascetic appearance and if the hair had been loose, the result would have been positively biblical. Like Morwenna, he wore a gold ankh, only in his case, it hung from one ear. The judge's rosette on all this fancy dress looked oddly ordinary.

Linus had little interest in the judging beyond that of seeing how a friend got on. He had no specialized knowledge of the breed and, apart from variations in colour and markings, would have been hard put to it to tell one from another. The people were far more interesting than the dogs and he found himself mentally placing the handlers in the order of their apparent professionalism. At the bottom went those who held the end of the lead and chatted to someone at the ringside. At the top went those whose entire attention was focused on their charge of the moment. Both Helen and Morwenna came into this category.

Helen had entered two dogs—one of them a puppy—and a bitch. They were beautifully presented and handled but Linus had no idea how a distinterested expert would have rated their quality. In each of their classes, they were second to a dog handled by Morwenna and in the classes in which Helen was not entered the first three were always owned or bred by her rival. Admittedly, it was statistically valid since Morwenna's stock predominated heavily but all the same, it looked bad to an outsider like Linus. He acknowledged that he was not a disinterested observer and that, had the judge had a more conventional appearance and looked less as if he shared Morwenna's wardrobe, it would not have looked so much like a 'fix'. However, he heard no sounds of disgruntlement from the ringside so maybe the judging wasn't so bad. He was pleased to notice that Helen made a point of congratulating the victor with every appearance of sincerity. No doubt when she got home she'd be kicking the cat and throwing things at the larder door, but that didn't matter.

'I'm sorry you didn't do better,' he said quietly as he accompanied her back to the benching tent.

She smiled. 'So am I, but not surprised. When I saw who the substitute judge was, I knew where the top awards would go.'

'I didn't hear any ringside grumbling,' Linus told her.

'You wouldn't. For one thing, once they saw who was judging, they'd all be resigned to it anyway and for another, they can't be sure who's listening.'

Linus wasn't entirely sure whether Helen meant the implication he read into her last remark and hoped she didn't. However, if she did, this was neither the time nor the place to ask her about it so he changed the subject.

'Would this be a good time to take up Chilson's invitation? Or, if we can't find him, to have a drink on our own account to compensate for the disappointment?'

'I'd like that.'

She settled her dogs back in their cages and another AVD exhibitor whom Helen introduced as Marion Curbridge and whom Linus privately classified as 'normal' expressed herself quite happy to keep an eye on them.

Linus half-hoped they wouldn't be able to find Chilson but in fact they quite literally bumped into him at the *Dog World* stand and were shepherded off to the bar, joining a table where the green ties of the men and the green-and-gold badges of the women told them they had joined an informal gathering of Kennel Club members. 'How did you do?' was the question addressed to them simultaneously, since no one knew which of them was the exhibitor.

'Second with each dog in its class,' Helen said.

'Disappointed?' one woman asked.

'Better than being thrown out with the rubbish,' Helen replied, and received a nod of approval.

'What's your breed?' someone inquired.

Helen told him.

'Vampire Dogs. Isn't that the breed with that Leyburn woman? I've never met her but she's quite an old witch, by all accounts. I bet she won.'

'She did, as a matter of fact, but it was a substitute judge. I've a feeling she wouldn't have had quite such an easy run otherwise,' Helen said.

'Was that one of Wingfield's breeds?' Chilson asked, and shook his head when Helen told him it was. 'Great pity, that. He was a good judge—of dogs, I mean. I don't think he ever looked at the other end of the lead. Fair-minded man, too. He had the makings of a very useful Club member.'

Helen looked surprised. 'I hadn't realized he belonged,' she said.

'He didn't, but his name had just been put forward. Pity it hadn't come up before, I suppose, but there's no point dwelling on that.'

'Do you ever judge those funny little things?' another man asked.

'Not yet,' Helen told him. 'I'd like to—I've had them about eight years now, if you count the time I had them in Mexico.' She smiled ruefully. 'I don't think my face fits, though.'

'You'd better invest in some ethnic robes and some amber beads, then you won't look so abnormally normal,' the woman who had asked if she were disappointed volunteered.

Helen grimaced. 'I think I prefer abnormality,' she said.

On their way back to the benching tent, Helen—whose disappointment had noticeably mellowed—said, 'You know, there are compensations to not going Best of Breed.'

'Are there? Do you catch many people refusing to accept it?' Linus asked.

'Don't be silly. What I mean is that if you go Best of Breed, you've more or less got to stay right till the very end to compete in the Group, which means there's a good chance of not getting away before six.'

'You didn't tell me that when you asked if I wanted to come,' Linus commented.

'As it is,' she went on, ignoring his remark, 'we can go home—' she looked at her watch—'in about an hour if we want to.'

'And do we want to?'

'I usually stay around and chat but today I think I'd prefer to get home earlier and perhaps cook you dinner.'

Linus was taken aback at the unexpectedness of the invitation.

'I'd like that,' he said. 'Are you sure it won't be too much trouble? I mean, it's been quite a tiring day.'

'If it were, I'd have kept my mouth shut,' she said.

She dropped Linus off at his home on Osney Island. This gave him a chance to feed his own dog, Ishmael, and take him for a walk while she saw to her animals and prepared the meal without the inconvenience of having to make conversation to a third party.

The storm that had been threatening all day, broke as Linus drove north. Great round-topped mountains of magnificently Wagnerian steel-blue storm-clouds piled up over the Cotswolds throwing an unnatural stillness and an uneasy clarity over the landscape. Put it on canvas, Linus thought, and even in the hand of a master it would be pure kitsch. In real life it was awe-inspiring and more than a little frightening. It was, in every sense of the word, a pregnant stillness and when parturition came, it did so with a head-splitting crash of thunder and a simultaneous sheet of lightning across the sky in front of him. The timing told him the storm was immediately overhead and by the time that fact had been acknowledged, the deluge was upon him with such force that he pulled over to the side of the road and hoped his hazard lights would be enough to warn any less cautious motorist. There was no visibility, not even with the windscreen wipers going at maximum speed on a stationary car, so Linus turned them off and sat there, cocooned in his warm, dry sanctuary.

Inevitably, the downpour eased, leaving the main road awash with sheets of water as the storm travelled further and further eastwards, taking its deluge with it. The state of the road gave him little opportunity to admire the clarity of the surrounding countryside or the beauty of the rainbow that now straddled it. Driving in these conditions was not fun and only the fact that he was more than half way to Long Blessington prevented him from turning round and going home to manufacture some plausible excuse.

Once he turned off the main road, conditions deteriorated and got steadily worse as he came nearer to his destination. Water-splashes in every dip in the road, some of them almost axle-deep, left him with no faith in his brakes which he sometimes had no chance to test before the next one came up. When he drew up in front of Helen's gate, his whole body sagged with relief at the easing of the tension that such concentrated driving had demanded.

Despite the warmth of the evening, Helen had lit a fire in the huge fireplace that dominated her sitting-room. Its heat was hardly necessary but the psychological effect was infinitely cheering.

'Come in and make yourself comfortable,' she said. 'I was half afraid you'd turn round and go home again if you were caught in the downpour. The roads must be appalling.'

'And forgo dinner with an attractive woman? Never,' he said, and meant it now that he was here, though he had the grace to be privately ashamed that she had so very nearly hit the nail on the head. 'And, yes, they are, especially the country ones. Every dip is a water-splash.'

'Is this area particularly liable to thunderstorms?' she asked.

Linus considered. 'I don't think so. Why?'

'This is the third since I moved here and that seems a lot. The others weren't anything like as heavy but they've all been more or less directly overhead.'

'I think it's more to do with the time of year,' Linus said. 'Storms are always more frequent in the summer.'

'But August, surely? Not June.'

'Maybe things are a little earlier this year. Are you afraid of them?'

She seemed surprised. 'No, not at all. In fact, I find them rather invigorating. Don't you?'

Linus thought about it. They certainly cleared the air and left a clean, fresh atmosphere behind them, but that wasn't what she meant. 'No, I don't think I do,' he said. 'In fact, if I'm absolutely honest, I don't much like them at all. I don't think I'm afraid of them, exactly, but they certainly make me ... apprehensive.'

Tacos were something new to Linus. He had never eaten Mexican food in his life and approached this dish with caution, the more so since he was obliged to eat it with his fingers. Helen had had the forethought to provide a mild sauce as well as a hot one but it wasn't long before Linus tried the latter and found he preferred it. She watched him ladling it on to the beef-stuffed taco shell before topping it with salad and cheese, and laughed.

'I can see you'll become a chili addict,' she said. 'I'll give you burritos next time.'

Linus enjoyed the meal and the wine that went with it: Helen's choice was several degrees up from mere plonk. The pudding—a syllabub—was refreshingly bad for him and so, he supposed, was the brandy that accompanied the coffee by the fire. He enjoyed the company, too. Helen made him feel at peace with himself and the world, though no doubt the wine and the brandy played their part, too. She also made him feel interesting and not like some anonymous government cipher, which he sometimes felt was his role in life. They sat by the fire for a long time and, if the conversation developed long pauses, they were mutually acceptable and didn't matter a bit.

CHAPTER THREE

Linus left in the morning feeling newer, younger and ready to tackle anything, feelings which were reinforced by the bright, clear light that always follows a storm. From the bedroom window he could see so far across the hills that he wouldn't have been surprised to learn that his view encompassed the proverbial five counties that are always attributed to extensive prospects.

A rook flew up from the gate-post as he approached it. It scarcely registered on Linus's consciousness. Three more on a fence opposite watched him get into his car and flew off when he turned the key. He noticed those and a shadow crossed his mood. After seeing what their fellows had done to Mr Justice Wingfield, he would never look at rooks in quite the same light again. There were several more on fences and overhanging branches lining the lane to Helen's house. Rooks were social birds, he reminded himself. They always congregate in numbers. What was it that stolid, unimaginative rural policeman had said of them? 'The messengers of the Dark'. Superstitious nonsense, of course, but all the same, Linus shivered. Then he put his foot down and returned to the sanity of the city.

A sudden influx of work and, in particular, several new instances of BSE left Linus with a pile of paperwork to catch up on and a disinclination to be sociable. He phoned Helen several times and knew she expected him to suggest dinner or lunch or an exhibition and he wanted to, but he felt that he would be poor company in his present mood and determined that he would repair the omission as soon as the workload slackened off a bit. Helen seemed to understand that he was working hard and it didn't cross his mind that she might think he was making excuses and letting her down lightly for some imagined disappointment of the night after Windsor. He did notice that her tone became increasingly reserved and she seemed rather abstracted during his later calls but he supposed she, too, had plenty to get on with and assumed that she therefore might actually be quite pleased not to be pestered with invitations for the present.

A second suspected case of BSE at Uppertop sent him out there. He determined before he got there that he would not look to see if there was still a scarecrow in the oatfield but as he drove past the bottom fence, his eyes were irresistibly drawn to the crown of the hill and he visibly relaxed when he saw that the skyline was empty of anything except oats.

There was no doubt about the diagnosis: the cow was ready to climb the wall of her loose-box when he, a stranger, came near. He told Tom he'd arrange for the lorry to collect her in three days' time and would be back to put her down a couple of hours before it was due. An impulse that sprang in part from a desire to take Tom's mind off his misfortune, if only for a few moments, made him say, 'Tom, you know Long Blessington. It's a pretty enough village.

Know anything about it?'

Tom Brigsteer smiled briefly. 'Pursuing the acquaintance with that young woman, are we? What do you want to know?'

'Nothing in particular, just general background,' Linus said, annoyed that he was too transparent. 'I got the impression when she mentioned it in the pub that you knew far more than you were saying.'

'Maybe I do. I don't know as there's much virtue in gabbing to complete strangers, do you?'

'Well, I'm not a complete stranger,' Linus told him, 'so gab to me.'

'You'd better come in and have a mug of tea.'

The farmer made the tea properly, in an old Brown Betty with a chipped spout, and put two mugs on the Formica work-top of a fitted kitchen that was probably the pride of Mrs Brigsteer's life. 'Help yourself,' he told Linus and Linus did.

'Very old village, Long Blessington,' he said, cradling his own mug between two huge hands.

Linus made no comment. The same could be said of most villages round here.

'Older than most. Much older,' Tom went on, as if he had been able to read Linus's thoughts. 'There's been a settlement there since Roman times at least. Farmers keep turning up bits of pavement and broken pots, and of course it's not too far from the standing stones so maybe it's even older than that. What I mean to say is,' he went on, determined that Linus should not miss the point, 'there's been some sort of village there since before Christianity. Folks as knows about these things reckon it dates back to the days of the Old Religion.'

He had lost Linus, who had only the haziest idea of what form religion took before Christianity if it wasn't in the Roman tradition. 'Celtic, do you mean? Or Roman?'

'Not Roman. I don't know about the other. I mean what you or me would probably call witchcraft. That's the religion of Long Blessington. Always was, always will be.'

Linus stared at him. 'You're having me on, Tom. You don't believe that rubbish.'

'I don't believe in it, no, but there's plenty as does—or so they say.'

'Come on, Tom. This is the twentieth century. There's a church in Long Blessington. An old one,' he added, as if that concluded the argument.

'Don't know what difference that's supposed to make. How many folks do you think turns up to church in this day and age? Not many, I can tell you.'

'Are you blaming falling church attendances on witchcraft?' Linus asked incredulously.

'No, of course I'm not. All I'm talking about is Long Blessington. That village has been associated with it since time began. There's plenty of recorded instances—and I'm not just talking about the mediaeval purges or the seventeenth-century hysteria. There were ritual killings of suspected witches in that village as late as the 'twenties. Did you know that?'

'I find it hard to believe.'

Tom shrugged. 'That's as maybe. You'll find it in the back issues of the local paper if you want the bother of looking. Funny thing, that: we hear about old ladies being brutally killed nowadays and we throw up our hands and say "How awful"—which it is, of course—and think it's a sign of our violent times, but the only thing new about it is that it's become an urban phenomenon. For centuries past it's always been a rural one.'

'That's the first time I've heard it suggested that the modern victims of mindless thugs were witches,' Linus said.

'I don't suppose the rural victims were, either. As often as not that was just the excuse. It doesn't mean there weren't witches, nor that there aren't still a few about. Quite a few, if what you read in the papers can be believed. Anyway, whatever the numbers, Long Blessington has always been regarded by the neighbouring villages as a hotbed of it. That's still said to be the case and there's no denying it attracts a funny sort of resident. They do say that incomers who aren't involved don't stay long.' He paused. 'Your lady-friend doesn't look like the usual run of Long Blessington weirdo.'

'She's not. She only moved there because the cottage was cheap as well as pretty.'

Tom nodded sagely. 'I seem to recall she said it was the one at the other end of the village, near the pond?'

Linus confirmed it.

Tom nodded again. 'Had several owners in recent years. I doubt if any of them stayed longer than a year, and when they got out, they got out in a hurry. Leastways, there was always a low asking price, and that's what it usually means.'

'I'd have thought the reason was more likely to be drains,' Linus remarked.

'Anywhere else, I'd agree. I'll tell you what: if you're sure your lady-friend's not one of them, I'd suggest she gets out and finds herself a cottage in a more congenial village. She hasn't been there long. She might as well go before it gets unpleasant.'

'Unpleasant? In what way?'

'How should I know? What I do know is that they'll go on getting people out until it's bought by one of their own.'

'I'm sorry, Tom, but this doesn't make sense,' Linus told him. 'If the price is so low, what's to stop them tipping off "one of their own", as you put it, and getting them in?'

Tom thought about that. 'Country cottages

round here cost the earth,' he said finally. 'Even when they're below market price, they're not exactly cheap. I don't doubt they pass the word, but the word's not going to be much use without the cash, is it?'

There was no disputing that and it was a very thoughtful Linus Rintoul who got back into his car.

When he reached the main road, he hesitated and then turned left towards Long Blessington instead of right towards Oxford. He glanced at his watch. He had no idea what hours Helen worked but, whether she did mornings or afternoons, it was about lunch-time so there was a reasonable chance she would be at home. As he drew up outside the cottage he was pleased to see her car in the drive.

'I was passing,' he said when she opened the door. 'I gambled on your not being offended that I hadn't rung first.'

Her manner was cautious, but polite. 'Of course not. Come in. I was just having some lunch. It's only bread and cheese, but you're welcome to join me.'

Linus was a bit taken aback. It wasn't quite the greeting he had expected, not when he remembered the warmth of their last parting. 'Is anything wrong?' he said.

'No. Should there be?'

'Well, no. It's just that . . . well, I suppose I expected a warmer welcome.'

'Did you now? Tough. You sleep here—for what it's worth (which maybe isn't much in your eyes), the first man I've slept with since Peter died—and then I get a succession of phone calls asking how I am and pleading pressure of work, which sound to me like a let-down. Oh, very kindly done—let her down gradually, and all that—but a let-down just the same. Then you turn up unannounced and I'm expected to be delighted! I take it you've suddenly decided you're ready for a bit more of the other, is that it?'

'No!' Linus exclaimed. 'No, it isn't like that at all! I really did have a lot of work on. Depressing work. I suppose I could have shelved some of the paperwork if I'd really tried but I thought I'd be a miserable companion and the last thing I wanted was for you to find me a misery. It wasn't meant to be a let-down and it never crossed my mind that's how you'd see it.'

She looked at him suspiciously. 'Do you mean that? Yes, I think you do. How thick men are sometimes!' She smiled and Linus was pleased to observe that it was almost her old smile. 'Come and have some lunch.'

The French stick had been warmed in the oven which was enough in Linus's opinion, to turn a simple meal into haute cuisine. The cheese was Stilton, the butter unsalted and the pickle was his favourite. A lunch fit for a king, he thought with satisfaction.

'What finally brought you here?' she asked.

Linus hesitated. He could easily say he had come out here just to see her but she was bright enough to ask why he hadn't phoned first and, since he certainly would have done had that been the case, the lie wouldn't stand up. Besides, he didn't like lying if it could be avoided. 'I was at Tom Brigsteer's—you know, the farmer I was with when you were looking for a vet. Your name came up and I thought it was about time I popped over. Sometimes one forgets how quickly time passes.'

'Very flattering. Dare I ask just how my name happened to pop up?'

'We were talking about Long Blessington. Tom put two and two together and assumed my interest was because of my acquaintance with you.'

Helen looked puzzled. 'What was so interesting about Long Blessington?'

'You told me the house had been very cheap. There's nothing that happens within a twenty-mile radius of Uppertop that Tom Brigsteer doesn't know all about. I thought he might know why.'

'And did he?'

'Yes.'

'Well?'

Linus fidgeted uncomfortably. How did one trained scientist tell another some yarn about witchcraft and expect not to be laughed out of the house? It served him right for trying to be honest. 'There's some cock-and-bull story about this village's having historical connections with witchcraft. He seems to think there's a lot of it about still and that outsiders aren't welcome to Long Blessington unless they're involved. His theory is that the people who have had this cottage were made to feel so uncomfortable that they left in a hurry and that they'll go on doing that until the cottage is sold to one of "them".'

Helen stared at him. 'I've never heard such nonsense. I hope you told him to go and sleep it off.'

'Well, no. Not exactly,' Linus said apologetically. 'In fact I more or less left him with the impression that I'd try to persuade you to leave.'

'Linus, there's no secret about Long Blessington's history. I'm only surprised you've not heard about it before. The story about outsiders isn't new, either. I heard it before I bought the place. I expect he mentioned the Vampire Dog people, too, in that connection.'

'As a matter of fact, he didn't,' Linus said. 'Mind you, if they go about their everyday affairs in that extraordinary get-up, I don't think you can blame anyone for assuming they've got something to do with it.'

Helen nodded. 'I've heard it mentioned in the village. It's all nonsense, of course. They're not very friendly and I've come to the conclusion that they're only interested in fair and unbiased judging if it happens to bring their dogs out on top. Apart from that, I think the only explanation for their rather distinctive way of dressing is that it plays up to the name of the breed. Like that girl in the Dracula evening-suit. You must have noticed her?'

Linus had and Helen's theory made perfectly good sense. On the other hand, Tom Brigsteer was neither imaginative nor inventive and, although Linus found it very hard to go along with the farmer's beliefs, there was no denying they were strongly held. 'All the same, it might not be a bad idea to look around for somewhere else,' he said.

'I've only just got here!' she exclaimed. 'No, Linus. This cottage suits me very well indeed and I've no intention of going to all the trouble and expense of moving again when I've only just got settled. In any case, there's no need. No one's trying to get me out—except you, I suppose. It's all psychological, you know: if you don't believe in witchcraft—and I don't—it can't work against you. It's as simple as that.'

Linus didn't believe in it either, but neither did he share Helen's simplistic faith. Still, it wasn't worth an argument, especially when his relationship with her was on somewhat unstable ground. He changed the subject. 'How are the dogs?' he asked.

She didn't at first realize there had been a change of topic. 'Oh, come, now. You're not suggesting . . . ? No, you're not. I'm sorry. They're fine. Well, a lot more perky though not perhaps right back to what they were. David Thelwall's very good and his treatment seems to be working, but it's taking its time.'

'Good. I thought you'd be happy with him.' Linus drank his coffee and then studied the bottom of his mug very intently. 'I don't suppose . . . I mean, are you feeling sufficiently forgiving to have dinner with me?'

Helen pursed her lips and drew her breath in sharply. 'Ooh, I don't know about that.'

Linus pushed his mug away and stood up. 'No, well, I can't blame you, I suppose. No harm in asking, though.'

'None at all—and do sit down, you idiot, unless you really have to rush off. I was only joking. I'd love to have dinner with you. I'm only sorry the invitation has been a long time coming.'

Linus looked at her and smiled and it struck Helen that on the rare occasions when his natural gravitas vanished, he looked quite boyish and rather vulnerable. 'Tomorrow?' he asked.

'Tomorrow would be fine,' she replied and, since it seemed he was determined to go now, she led the way to the door. 'By the way, I had a letter the other day and I've been bursting ever since to tell someone about it.'

'Then tell me.'

'I've been invited to judge Vampire Dogs! My first judging appointment! Isn't that great? It's only four classes—they're scheduling them for the first time. It's something of an experiment and they've slotted them in at rather short notice, which is why they've asked me so close to the date. I'm over the moon.'

'Did you accept?'

'Did I . . . ? You're pulling my leg. Yes, Linus, I accepted—and without a second thought.'

'Then it's a good job I invited you out to dinner: this calls for a celebration. I'll pick you up at half past seven.'

* * *

Linus booked a table at the Old George at Leafield. It was sufficiently far from Long Blessington for him to be reasonably sure she wouldn't know it, small enough to be intimate, and had a menu that contained several old faithfuls in case she wasn't adventurous and at least as many unusual dishes to choose from if she were. He thought it likely that anyone who had lived in Mexico and dared to offer a Mexican dish to a man on their first date would come into the latter category and was pleased to be proved right. Food was, in Linus's opinion, one of the great delights of life and a woman who opted for something she cooked every week at home was not likely to hold his interest for very long.

Linus took little notice of the other diners and none at all in new arrivals, so he was surprised that one of them should pause by his and Helen's table on his way to his own. He looked up and found Inspector Lacock, a policeman with whom he had a more than passing acquaintance, looking from him to her and back again with considerable interest.

'Good evening, Rintoul. Mrs Glenbarr,' he said.

'You know each other?' Linus asked, surprised.

'We've met,' Lacock conceded. 'How are you, Mrs Glenbarr?'

'Fine, thank you, Inspector. Are you alone?'

'No. My wife's powdering her nose. You've had no problems?'

Helen seemed bemused. 'Everyone has problems of one sort or another, Inspector. Is that a personal inquiry or a professional one?'

'No unpleasant letters? Threatening phone calls?'

'No, none. There was the one during the trial, but you knew about that. There's been nothing since, thank goodness. I never did think a humble lab technician would be a serious target.' She turned to Linus. 'The

Inspector was on that case I told you about: the one that judge presided over.'

'I was beginning to put two and two together,' Linus said.

'All the same,' Lacock went on, 'let us know if there is anything. After all, Wingfield's dead and we'd rather there were no more fatalities.'

'Don't worry, Inspector. You'll be the first to know. As a matter of fact, we're just celebrating my own elevation to the ranks of judges.'

Lacock looked at her blankly. 'How come?'

'Dogs,' she explained. 'I've got my first judging appointment. Four classes of Amazonian Vampire Dogs. I'm quite excited.'

'Congratulations. Isn't that those funny little dogs that peculiar woman at Long Blessington has?' Linus had the impression that Lacock was trying to put Helen's information into some sort of context.

'I live there, too,' Helen commented, 'so I hope you mean Morwenna Leyburn.'

'That's the name. I hope you've got a crucifix to wear. To judge by local gossip, you'll need it.' He glanced at Linus. 'I'd make sure you wear your seat-belt when you're out with him, too. He's got quite a track record for accidents.' A woman whom they took to be Mrs Lacock joined the Inspector and paused expectantly. 'Enjoy your meal,' the policeman concluded, steering her towards their own table.

'What a strange thing to say,' Helen

commented. 'You've struck me as a very responsible driver.'

'That isn't quite what he meant. I've been caught up a couple of times in things that sort of impinge on Lacock's area, that's all. I think the remark was his idea of a joke.'

Nevertheless, Lacock's comments seemed to have left a shadow across the celebration which his departure did nothing to lift. Linus pushed his venison steak around the plate. 'This witchcraft business seems to be general knowledge,' he said.

'Rubbish. Tom Brigsteer—a man who's lived in the area all his life—and a police inspector have heard of it. That hardly makes it general knowledge. I should think any policeman worth his salt would pick up all sorts of odds and ends of rumour like that, wouldn't you?'

'I suppose so.' The agreement was grudging. Somewhere at the back of his mind Linus recalled the words of that stolid and apparently unimaginative policeman when he had noticed the rooks. When bizarre events were treated lightly, they didn't matter. When they seemed to be taken seriously by otherwise balanced and unneurotic individuals, he found himself feeling uneasy. The venison completed another couple of circuits. 'All the same,' Linus said at last, 'I think it might be a good idea to think about moving.'

Helen finished her salmon and wiped her

mouth carefully and deliberately. 'Linus, let's get one thing absolutely clear. I like you. I enjoy your company. That—and one night together—does not authorize you to pressurize me into doing something I don't want to do. I've already told you that I can't afford to move again so soon, even if I wanted to—and I'm not at all sure that I do want to. On this particular subject I think you're being superstitious and mediaeval. Whatever happened to reason? I'm no more likely to be influenced by someone muttering about eye of newt than a humble lab technician is to be threatened for her part in ensuring a well-deserved conviction. So drop it, please.'

She didn't add, 'Or I'll drop you,' but Linus had the impression it was implicit in her command. The irritating thing was that he knew she was right. His intellect agreed with everything she said. Unfortunately, it wasn't his intellect that had the upper hand. It was a gut feeling that had nothing to do with intellect.

He smiled, but it cost him an effort. 'I'll try. I know perfectly well I've no right to interfere. It's just that . . . well, maybe I'm speaking out of turn, but I do care. The way anyone would care about a friend,' he added hastily, unwilling to risk her reading more into his words than he intended.

She smiled, apparently effortlessly. 'Which reminds me,' she said. 'One should always thank friends for services rendered, don't you think? I told you I'd had this judging invitation. I didn't tell you it was thanks to you.'

'Me? How can it be thanks to me? I've no influence over dog shows.'

'Not directly, perhaps. Do you remember at Windsor we had drinks with your Kennel Club friend, John Chilson, and some others?' Linus nodded. 'Well, the secretary of the society that's invited me to judge is the woman who advised me to invest in some ethnic robes and amber beads. Remember?'

Linus did, but only vaguely. He would not have been able to describe the woman. 'I think so,' he said cautiously.

'I can only conclude that when the idea of scheduling AVDs came up, she recalled the conversation and decided to put my name forward. Whatever the reason, I don't think it would have happened if you hadn't been with me—so thank you.'

'Think nothing of it,' Linus said. 'Any time. All you have to do is ask.'

She put her head on one side and looked at him speculatively. 'Do you mean that?'

'Ye . . . es.' Linus's tone was wary.

'Good. Then would you be willing to come with me? I know it's not really your scene, but I would like some moral support.'

Linus was quietly pleased to be asked. He got out his diary. 'When is it?' he said and duly marked the date, some six weeks hence. 'One of the advantages of being a civil servant is that, barring an outbreak of foot-and-mouth or rabies, at least I can make appointments with a reasonable expectation of keeping them.'

'There was one other thing,' she went on, and paused.

'Yes?'

'I was hoping you'd come back home with me tonight.'

Linus's surprise was evident. 'Of course I will. We came in my car, remember?'

'That wasn't quite what I meant.'

'Oh,' Linus said. He paused while he digested it. 'Oh, I see.' He grinned. 'That sounds like an admirable idea. You're sure?'

'I'd have been a fool of some magnitude to suggest it if I weren't,' Helen pointed out.

CHAPTER FOUR

Linus saw a lot of Helen in the ensuing weeks and took very good care not to let any amount of work interfere with arrangements they had made or put him in a position where he wasn't free to make arrangements. Neither of them referred to the bone of contention that they had come close to fighting over. Linus became almost used to the tiny little dogs and their peculiar habit of running along the back of the sofa to sit on one's shoulder. He guessed that, in the crook of the shoulder and neck, they found the warmth that their little bodies probably needed. Despite their abundant coats, the heat-loss from such a relatively large surface area must be considerable. Far more disconcerting was their habit of licking the neck of their host. Linus told himself it was almost certainly nothing more than social grooming. Still, he could quite see how they got their name.

He was pleased to discover that Helen's dogs did not monopolize her entire attention or her entire conversation and he was perfectly happy, as the date of her judging appointment drew closer, to test her on the Breed Standard much as he had once tested his son on the Highway Code.

Two weeks before the show, he came home to find a deceptively calm message on his answering machine. It was Helen telling him that she had found one of her dogs dead when she came down that morning and another had been dead when she had come back from work. She added that she would be very grateful if he could go over to Long Blessington that evening. She wanted to talk to someone.

Linus went over as soon as he had fed and exercised Ishmael. It was obvious that Helen had spent the greater part of the day in tears and when she opened the door to him and he put his arms round her, she burst into tears with renewed vehemence that he made no attempt to staunch.

Not until her tears had abated somewhat did he leave her to make coffee, taking care to lace hers with a generous slurp of brandy.

'Drink this,' he said, 'and then tell me all about it. Where are they?'

Correctly interpreting this as a reference to the two dogs she told him they were over at Thelwall's. 'As soon as I found Mouse this morning and realized there was no obvious reason for his death, I took him over for a post-mortem. Then I came home and found Tipsy dead, so of course, I took her over as well.'

'They hadn't seemed ill yesterday?'

'No, not really. They've been under the weather along with the others, but you know about that—and in any case, they've been much better lately. I wonder if it's a serious recurrence of that? If it is I could lose the lot.'

'No bloody diarrhoea with a highly offensive smell?' Linus persisted.

'We don't think it's parvo,' she said. 'Nothing like that. That's the whole point, there's been nothing that one can describe as a symptom. Nothing at all.'

'Then there's nothing you can do except wait for the results of Thelwall's post-mortem,' he told her. 'Has he seen the others yet?'

'No. I was going to take them over this evening for a check-up.'

'I'll do it now, if you like—not instead of taking them to Enstone, because he's more up-to-date on small animals than I am, but it will give you a preliminary opinion.'

Linus could find nothing wrong with the little dogs. Their temperatures were normal, their colour a healthy pink, their eyes bright and palpation revealed no abnormalities. It seemed likely that, in the absence of any more specific indications of ill-health, Thelwall would probably prescribe another course of antibiotics, but different ones this time, in case their systems had become too accustomed to the previous one.

David Thelwall concurred with Linus's diagnosis. The post-mortems had revealed nothing at all and he asked Helen if she wanted them sent off for a full autopsy. Helen hesitated and then agreed to it. 'I'd hoped to know what it was in case the others go down with it,' she said. 'An autopsy will take days. Still, we need to know.'

'I think it's a wise decision,' Linus told her. 'It may indicate a line of prevention we can try. By your own admission they die without any previous warnings so there's no question of being able to treat early symptoms.'

Back at the cottage, Helen re-arranged the

dog's sleeping-boxes so that they were all in her bedroom. 'I'm not leaving anything to chance,' she told Linus. 'At least this way if there is the slightest sound, I'll hear it.'

'Do you want me to stay the night?' he asked doubtfully.

She managed a smile. 'Not really. I'm not in the mood and besides, every time a dog turns round, I'll be jumping up to see if it's all right. Quite apart from its being no fun for you, you won't get a lot of sleep. If you don't mind something out of the freezer, I'm quite happy to give you a meal.'

It wasn't the most gracious of invitations but Linus didn't mind that and he had a feeling that it would be better for Helen if she were not thrown entirely on her own resources for a while, so he accepted with perfectly genuine alacrity and discovered that 'something out of the freezer' did not mean a ready-made meal in a foil dish, but a full-scale toad-in-the-hole of which only the toad and the green vegetables had any connection with the freezer at all.

While Linus ate with some gusto, Helen picked at hers with a noticeable lack of appetite that made him feel a little guilty that he had accepted her offer of a meal. Then he told himself that she would probably have eaten nothing at all if she hadn't cooked for him and that he had therefore done her a service. Her loss of appetite was understandable but she had been breeding dogs for long enough to have encountered unexpected losses before. It might have been the loss of two dogs in such quick succession that resulted in the peculiar effect, or there might have been something else.

'Are you sure you're all right?' he asked eventually.

She shrugged. 'A bit low, that's all. I'll get over it.'

'There isn't anything else?'

'Such as?'

'I don't know, really. You would let the police know if you had any unpleasant phone calls or letters, wouldn't you?'

'Of course I would.'

'And have you had?'

'No.' She gave up her half-hearted efforts to eat her meal. 'Linus, I've lost two very dear dogs in inexplicable circumstances and I'm terrified I'll lose the rest before we find out what killed them. You hear about these things from time to time, but you don't expect them to happen to you and when they do it's a very nasty shock. It's also very upsetting. I shan't feel any easier until we get the autopsy results back, and only then if I haven't lost any more. I don't expect to be cross-questioned about all sorts of other highly improbable causes for my low spirits.'

'I'm sorry: it wasn't supposed to be cross-questioning. I'm concerned about you, that's all.'

'And now I'm supposed to be terribly sorry for having jumped down your throat and terribly grateful for your concern, I suppose? Well, I'm not. No, that's not strictly true. It's nice that you're concerned, and it's typical of you because you're a nice man, but I don't want your concern. Your company, your support—yes, those are both welcome but not your concern. It implies too much. More than I'm prepared to accept right now.'

'I see,' said Linus, who didn't.

'No, you don't. You're just hurt, and for that I'm sorry. Linus, I *do* enjoy your company but just lately it's been a little too easily available. I need a little space, a little time. I'm not saying that I don't want to see you again—I'd be very sorry if I didn't, but couldn't we leave it for a while? Give it a break?'

Linus felt stunned. Why had he had no inkling that she felt like this? He tried to convince himself that it was just another facet of the shock she had experienced this morning but he had a feeling that the only effect the shock had had was to give her the strength to say it.

'If that's how you feel, then I suppose we'd better,' he said, surprised that his voice seemed to betray no hint of his own feelings.

'Good. I'm glad you see it like that. I'm afraid there's only ice-cream for a pudding. Will that do?'

Linus said it would but he would have been quite unable, had anyone asked him, to tell them what flavour or even what colour it had been. He declined coffee. There was something about coffee, which they always had in the sitting-room, sitting side by side on the sofa, that introduced a note of intimacy that seemed no longer appropriate. He made an early start at the stockyard his excuse and noticed that Helen didn't query it.

He paused at the door. 'This show you've got coming up,' he said. 'The judging appointment, I mean. Will you still want some moral support?'

'If you're not too offended to provide it,' she told him. 'Give me a ring a couple of days beforehand and we'll fix it up.'

Back in his Osney Island cottage, Linus made himself the coffee he had previously declined and laced it heavily with whisky. Later, when the feeling of total failure had finally sunk in, he would progress to plain whisky. To say he was shattered by Helen's ultimatum was an understatement of the utmost magnitude and he had a shrewd suspicion that, despite her readiness to have his company at the forthcoming show, this evening had really seen the beginning of the end. Since he had no idea where he had gone wrong, he could formulate no plan for putting it right. He hadn't ever tried to analyse his feelings for Helen and, now that it seemed a good time for doing so, he found it very difficult.

He was a man of carefully fostered eccentricities but underneath them, he was conventional. He enjoyed the company of women but it rarely came his way for the simple reason that he was not very good at initiating an acquaintance. It was an area in which he had a diffidence that didn't extend to any other field of activity. If he envisaged a long-term relationship with a woman at all, it would be within marriage and he was forced to admit to himself that he had never slipped into the habit of seeing Helen in the role of his wife. That omission had never struck him before. Now that it did, he supposed it must have some significance, though whether the significance lay in what it might reveal about his deeper feelings for her or whether it spoke more about his lack of self-confidence in his dealings with women, he couldn't decide.

His marriage had broken up for a number of reasons, prominent among them being what his wife called his unreliability. He knew this was no personal failing, but due to the exigencies of being a vet in general practice, and for that reason he had given up in favour of the more stable hours of a Ministry vet. It hadn't saved the marriage because it hadn't been the real problem, but years of being told he was unreliable had had their inevitable effect and it now looked as if, in his efforts not to provoke the same criticism from Helen, he had been too readily available. She had said she wanted space. That meant she felt confined, constrained by their friendship. She had felt she was being smothered while he had simply been happy in what he had seen as a close and fulfilling friendship. His complete lack of awareness of any hint as to how she felt made him berate himself for an insensitive moron, even though a concentrated retrospection threw up no hindseen insights into how Helen must have been feeling.

The second whisky had him feeling sorry for himself. The third made him defiant but, even as he climbed the stairs vowing he'd show her how much he didn't need her company, he was not so drunk that he didn't recognize it was the alcohol talking, and in the morning he just felt glum.

It proved quite easy to immerse himself in his work again, and he did so successfully, with only a passing thought for Helen, and that related more to the cause of the dogs' death. It was a professional curiosity which a phone call to Thelwall would have satisfied. Unfortunately, professional ethics precluded such a call without Helen's express permission and, although he had no doubt at all that she would give it if he asked, he was loath to ring her. She would be bound to interpret such a call as an excuse to get in touch again. If he should happen to bump into Thelwall, it would be perfectly easy to say, 'By the way ...' and Thelwall, knowing of his friendship with Helen, would almost certainly tell him. Since he wasn't likely to bump into him and would have no reason to visit the quarantine kennels in the foreseeable future, he would have to remain in ignorance. If he decided to keep his promise and take Helen to the show—and he was by no means sure that this would be a good idea—he would ask her and then, with her permission, get a fuller, more technical account from her vet.

He did toy briefly once or twice with the idea of inviting her for a meal but fear of a tactfully worded refusal stopped him. She had said she still wanted his company at the show. Very well, he would keep to his intention of not contacting her at all until a couple of days beforehand. Then he'd play it by ear. If it seemed an invitation would not be entirely unwelcome, he'd make one, taking care to let it sound off-hand, so that she wouldn't think a refusal would hurt. It did strike him that there was a certain inconsistency in having decided on the one hand that he did not envisage his relationship with Helen becoming permanent and his fear of rejection by her on the other, but since he suspected that an analysis of this ambivalence might not reflect entirely to his credit, he chose not to consider it further.

Two days before Helen's judging engagement he telephoned her. Instead of giving her number when she picked up the receiver, there was a slight pause at the other end of the line and then a cautious, 'Yes?'

'Helen? Linus here. It is the day after tomorrow that you're judging, isn't it? Do you still want me to come with you?'

He wondered if it were just his imagination or whether she really did sound relieved. 'Yes, it is and yes, I'd like you to,' she said. 'I wasn't sure if you'd want to or whether you were too offended.'

'Why should I be offended?'

'Because I thought you were getting too serious too soon.'

'Oh, that. No, I wasn't offended,' he said with perfect truth because 'offended' was not the right word. 'It was very sensible—or so I came to realize. You're sure you want my company? You're not just being polite?'

'I'm quite sure. In fact, I've come close to calling you once or twice myself and then I thought perhaps I'd better not, perhaps it would be better to wait until you rang me.'

It was a promising start and Linus was loath to risk provoking another rebuff; still, nothing ventured and all that. 'I don't suppose you'd like dinner with me tonight or tomorrow,' he said and then, when he heard the hesitation at the other end, wished he hadn't.

'I'd like to, but I won't,' she said. 'It's nothing personal, truly it's not. It's just that . . . well, I've lost another dog. I don't want to leave them and, frankly, I'm not in the mood to cook for someone else or I'd invite you here.'

'I quite understand,' Linus said, disappointed. 'I'm sorry about the dog. I assume it was the same cause as the others? What exactly did the autopsy reveal?'

'Nothing. All it told us was that the dogs were dead, hardly an essential diagnosis in the circumstances. This third case is very similar and we are assuming it's the same, but that's not really much help when we don't know what the cause is in the first place.'

'How are you going to manage for the show? You'll be away all day,' Linus pointed out.

'I've got someone coming in to dog-sit. A friend. She's not remotely dog-minded, but that doesn't matter. She'll sit with them and not let them out and, if anything goes wrong she can get David Thelwall round here right away.'

'What time do you want me to pick you up?'

'Judging begins at ten, but I'm not first in the ring. All the same, I'd like to be there in good time. Let's say eight o'clock. Will that be OK?'

Linus shuddered silently. He had guessed it would mean an early start but had foolishly not thought to wonder just how early. If he picked Helen up at eight, he would have to leave home at seven-thirty and before he could leave home, there would be Ishmael to exercise, to say nothing of breakfast to cook, eat and wash up. In short, a six o'clock start at the very latest. 'Eight o'clock will be fine,' he said.

He put the phone down with a faint feeling of unease. Everything about Helen's conversation had been entirely normal—except the very beginning. She had answered the telephone as if she had been reluctant to do so at all, and certainly as if she had no intention of imparting any information that she didn't have to. He should have asked why and taken a chance on being told it was nothing to do with him.

Back at Government Buildings he spoke to one of the secretaries about it. She pursed her lips. 'I dare say she's been getting funny phone calls,' she suggested. 'They're supposed to pick numbers at random so the secret is not to give your own, then they can't be sure of dialling it again.'

'That's horrible!' Linus exclaimed, aghast.

'Yes, isn't it?' the girl agreed savagely. 'One of the hazards of being a woman and neither the police nor the telephone people care two hoots about it. Oh, they make sympathetic noises, but they don't do anything helpful except suggest you change your number or go ex-directory, which is hardly practical for most people.'

'You sound as if you speak from experience,' Linus commented.

'That's right.'

'Maybe I'd better ring her and find out.'

'I shouldn't. If she's had more than one, her stomach will turn over as soon as it rings. Why subject her to that? Wait till you see her and ask her about it then.'

Her advice made sense and Linus followed it, though reluctantly. His resolve wavered once or twice and his hand reached out for the phone, but Lisa had known what she was talking about so each time he withdrew it. Two days was not very long, after all.

* * *

He pulled up in front of Helen's gate at a punctilious five to eight, and frowned. The cottage had that odd, inexplicably flat look that houses always do have when their occupants are absent and he automatically checked his watch—not just the time depicted but the tick, together with a cross-reference to the dashboard clock. Five to eight. He walked up the path and knocked on the door. A dog yapped inside and another one joined in but no one came to the door.

Linus knocked again with the same result and then went round to the back of the house, peering through windows as he went. He could see nothing untoward downstairs and there was no response to the generous hammering he gave the kitchen door, except a more prolonged yapping from the dogs who were in the cages by the boiler in which he knew they had spent the night.

Finding no response from the house itself, Linus pushed up the garage door. Helen's car had gone. He relaxed. She'd probably popped along to the village shop for something she'd forgotten, he thought, and almost immediately remembered that it was only eight o'clock. More probably she had gone to fetch the dog-sitter. That meant she wouldn't be long. He'd turn the car round and wait for her.

Within five minutes a rather rackety yellow and green Diane came to a tinny halt at the garage door and a rather earnest young woman in a pink jogging suit that was definitely not her colour got out and reached into the back to collect a bulging sports bag. She walked up the path and had let herself in before Linus had had time for her intention to register.

He dashed up the path in her wake and knocked. A puddingy and deeply suspicious face peered round the door at him.

'Yes?' it said.

'I'm Linus Rintoul. I'm supposed to be taking Helen to her show. I don't suppose you know where she is?'

'On her way, I imagine. Has her car gone?'

'Yes, it has. I thought maybe she'd gone to collect her dog-sitter. There didn't seem to be anyone in and she did say someone was going to stay with them.'

The unprepossessing female relaxed very slightly. 'I'm the dog-sitter,' she said. 'I told her I'd be here as close to eight as I could manage but she knows I'm not very good at getting up. That's why I had a key. Are you sure she was expecting you?'

'Quite sure.' There was no doubt in Linus's mind about that and he knew there could have been none in Helen's. 'I don't suppose she's left a note?' he asked.

'I haven't seen one but then I haven't looked.' She hesitated. 'I'm sorry, but I'm going to shut you out while I have a look,' she said. 'I'm sure you're who you say you are, but this isn't my house and you can't be too careful these days.'

Linus assured her that he quite understood and waited with growing impatience while she fulfilled her promise. He had no doubt her search would be thorough but she didn't give the impression of being someone who worked quickly.

'Nothing,' she said when her head finally reappeared round the front door. 'Nothing remotely resembling a note for you or anyone else—well, except for the feeding instructions, but that's quite straightforward. Perhaps you were late and she just gave up waiting.'

'Actually I was five minutes early,' Linus said

testily. He rather prided himself on his punctuality and resented having it impugned, particularly by a complete stranger.

The woman shrugged. 'I can't help, then,' she said. 'Obviously she decided to go earlier for some reason. Maybe you'd better just follow on to the show and sort it out with her there.'

It began to sound as if she had changed her mind about having his company after all, Linus thought bitterly. He certainly wasn't driving over a hundred miles to be told so. 'I'll leave her a note,' he said. 'Have you any paper? And an envelope,' he added. He had no great desire to have his note read and speculated upon to pass the dog-sitter's time.

'I'll have a look,' she said and closed the door once more.

When she reappeared, she handed him a jotter and a roll of Sellotape. 'No envelopes,' she said, 'and no scissors. You'll have to use your teeth, but this will do to seal it. Pop it through the letter-box when you've finished and I'll prop it up on the mantelpiece where Helen's sure to see it.' She closed the door.

Not a trusting soul, Linus thought as he took the paper and sticky tape back to his car. Still, that's not necessarily a bad thing these days. It wasn't easy to compose a note which was devoid of the mixture of annoyance and hurt he felt, but he managed it, confining himself to informing her that he had arrived on time and had been sorry to find that she had apparently decided to go on without him, and that he would have appreciated a phone call to let him know she had changed her mind. He posted the sealed note and the Sellotape through the letter-box and drove back to Oxford, uncertain whether to be sorry for himself, angry with Helen, or glad to be rid of the necessity of wondering whether the friendship would be revived.

He was too annoyed with the unsatisfactoriness of the morning to settle to doing anything useful or relaxing, so he took Ishmael for a long walk along the canal bank and on to Portmeadow. The dog could hardly believe his luck and, since there were by some miracle, no other dogs on the meadow at the time, he was able to run free.

A police car outside his house awaited their return.

As he fitted his key in the door, Detective-Inspector Netley climbed out and came over to him, his sergeant at his heels. 'You've been a long time, Mr Rintoul,' he said.

'I took the dog for a walk,' Linus told him and resisted with some difficulty the temptation to ask if there were now a law against it. Netley was not the sort of policeman who would smile.

'Without your car?'

'It was a walk, Inspector. Those don't usually involve cars.'

'Yes, I am aware of that, sir,' the policeman said with the heavy irony of one addressing a mildly intransigent adolescent. 'I was just surprised that you didn't use the car to get to wherever you wanted to walk the dog.'

'We walked along the towpath from Hythe Bridge Street to Portmeadow,' Linus explained patiently. 'Parking in this city is either expensive or non-existent, though I suppose the regulations don't bother your lot. It was easier to walk the whole way. Satisfied?'

'Perfectly. May we come in?'

Linus privately pushed the Inspector one notch higher in his admittedly low estimation for ignoring the bait he had cast. 'Of course,' he said. Then, when he had closed the door behind them, he asked, 'I take it there's been a development in the business concerning the scarecrow?'

'Why should you assume that, sir?' the Inspector inquired.

Linus chided himself for not having remembered that policemen, like psychiatrists, always seem to answer one question with another. 'As far as I know, it's our only area of common interest.'

'Precisely, sir—as far as you know. Are you acquainted with a certain—' he paused while he consulted his notebook—'A certain Helen Glenbarr?'

Linus had the unpleasant sensation that the

Copernican calculations had suddenly been reversed. 'I do know someone of that name,' he admitted cautiously, knowing that there was very little statistical likelihood of there being another in the area.

'And where does your Helen Glenbarr live?' Detective-Inspector Netley persisted.

Linus told him.

'When did you last see her?'

Linus calculated. 'About a fortnight ago. Perhaps a little more. David Thelwall will be able to tell you more precisely because she had been to him that morning.'

'You haven't seen her since then?'

'No. I have spoken to her on the telephone, though.'

'Ah.' The Detective-Inspector's interest increased. 'When would that have been?'

'The day before yesterday.'

'Would you care to tell me what it was about?'

'Not particularly,' Linus said tartly. 'It wasn't particularly private, however, so there's no good reason for not telling you. I wanted to ask her whether she still wanted me to take her to a dog show. It was her first judging engagement in this country and she had originally said she'd like a bit of moral support.'

'From which I deduce that you thought she might have changed her mind?'

Linus hesitated. 'Well, yes; we'd decided to

see a little less of each other for a while.'

'Her idea or yours?'

Linus hesitated again. No man—probably no woman, either, he thought suddenly—likes to admit being given the brush-off. 'Hers,' he admitted. 'She'll confirm it, I'm sure.'

'Were you upset by that decision?'

'At the time I suppose I was, but it wore off.'

'I see. You decided you could do without her.'

'No, not exactly. I decided I liked her company—liked it rather well, to tell the truth—but I didn't want it to turn into something permanent. That may come, of course, but not yet.'

Netley made no comment. 'Did she still want your support at the show?' he asked.

'Yes. I was to pick her up at eight o'clock this morning.'

The policeman looked at his watch. 'Short dog show,' he commented.

'I didn't go. Oh, I turned up, all right, but she'd gone. She must have changed her mind. There was a dog-sitter there. She let me leave a note.'

'I don't suppose you know whether you were on time or not? Eight o'clock, I think you said.'

'I arrived at precisely seven fifty-five.'

'Precisely?'

'Yes, Inspector. I tend to be extremely punctual. In this case I double-checked my watch and the dashboard clock when I realized the house was empty.'

'I thought you said there was a dog-sitter there?'

'There was, but she arrived a few minutes after I did. I don't know how many,' Linus went on, anticipating the next question. 'I'd had time to peer in the windows and walk round the back to see if there was any sign of life there.'

'Was there?'

'No, only the dogs. Inspector, don't you think you'd better tell me what all this is about?'

The Detective-Inspector ignored the question. 'Is this the note you left?'

Linus looked at it and nodded. 'Yes.'

'And where did you leave it?'

'I didn't. I posted it through the letter-box. The dog-sitter said she'd put it on the mantelpiece. I've no idea whether she did or not.'

'She did. Mr Rintoul, are you quite sure you didn't see Helen Glenbarr at any time between, say, yesterday tea-time and the time you reached the cottage?'

'Absolutely sure.'

'And where was this dog show?'

'Newark—at the county agricultural showground.'

'Then can you suggest why Mrs Glenbarr

should have gone to Silbury Hill?'

'Silbury Hill?' Linus echoed. 'But that's in the opposite direction! Why should she have gone there?'

'I was hoping you could tell me, Mr Rintoul. You see, that's where we found Mrs Glenbarr's body.'

CHAPTER FIVE

Linus stared at him in stunned silence. Then he went over to the cupboard and poured himself a neat whisky which he downed in one gulp. He poured himself another and sat down with it. 'You mean Helen's dead?' he said as if there might have been a misunderstanding.

'I'm afraid so,' Netley told him. 'The body was spotted by an army helicopter soon after dawn this morning. It was spreadeagled on top of the hill—and it was quite naked.'

'But you were able to identify her?'

'There's an engraving on the inside of her wedding-ring. Did you know that?' Linus shook his head. 'There's the very faint possibility that it may not be her wedding ring, but we're checking her dental records and we don't really think there's much doubt about it.'

'Was she murdered?' Linus asked.

'It's a possibility we're not inclined to

discount in the circumstances. We shan't know for sure until Forensic have finished. They're working on it now.'

Linus snorted. 'Ironic.'

'Ironic? In what way?'

'Helen was a lab technician—in a forensic laboratory. Surely you've discovered that?'

'We're aware of it, naturally. Were you aware of any condition that might lead to sudden death? Any depression?'

Linus shook his head. 'She never mentioned any illness and if she suffered from depression, she hid it well. She was a fairly recent widow, of course, but I formed the impression she had more or less come to terms with that. Even if there had been something—and I assume you're considering the possibility of suicide—it surely wouldn't have taken her to Silbury Hill and induced her to take her clothes off?'

'That doesn't strike you as being in character?'

'Quite the reverse, if anything. She wasn't noticeably unconventional.'

'You knew her well enough to be categorical about that?'

Linus found himself getting angry. 'Let me put it another way, Inspector. She wasn't the sort of woman who takes her clothes off at the drop of a hat.'

'Quite so, sir. Now, is there anything you'd like to tell us that might be relevant?'

'No, nothing. Wait a minute, though—you do know there's a connection between her and that judge who was discovered a few weeks ago?'

The policeman's notebook came out again, though its owner was not admitting ignorance of what might ensue. 'What connection is that, Mr Rintoul?'

'She gave evidence—forensic evidence, I mean—at the trial he presided over.'

'Had she had any threats?'

'I believe she had one during the trial but it was before I knew her so I heard about it afterwards. Inspector Lacock knows about it, so I suppose there must be a police record of it somewhere.'

'Had there been any threats since you met her?'

'She didn't tell me of any.'

'There is one other thing, Mr Rintoul. Was she on drugs?'

The question startled Linus by its unexpectedness. 'Good God, no! That's to say, I don't think so. No, I'm sure she wasn't.'

'How can you be quite so sure?'

Linus considered the matter. 'I can't, I suppose. Not absolutely.' He frowned. 'She and her husband had lived in Mexico, of course, and she did say something about there being marijuana in the mountains. I suppose she might have tried it. I certainly never had the slightest reason to think she might be smoking now. As a matter of fact, she didn't even smoke tobacco.'

'The two substances are not necessarily mutually exclusive,' the policeman said repressively. 'Nothing stronger? Heroin, for instance?'

'No,' Linus said emphatically. 'Why?'

'One theory is that she OD'd.'

'I don't believe it.'

'Then we'll have to wait for the forensic report, sir, won't we?'

Linus frowned. 'Even if it's positive, it doesn't necessarily mean it was self-administered,' he said.

'Quite so, sir,' the policeman said drily. 'That possibility had crossed our minds. If you've nothing more you can tell us, we'll be on our way but if you remember anything else—no matter how small—you know how to get hold of us?'

The question was rhetorical and the notebook snapped shut without waiting for a reply. The two policemen took their leave, promising Linus another visit from a minion who would require a statement.

Guilt was the emotion that predominated when the officers had left. Common sense told Linus that, even if he had arrived early that morning, Helen would still have been gone and that following her would have been quite impractical because there would still have been no way of knowing in which direction she had gone, much less her destination. Perhaps if he had pressed his dinner invitation, she might have told him if anything was worrying her. More usefully, he might have ended up spending the night again, with the possibility that whatever situation had arisen, she might have discussed it with him and, as a consequence, not have gone away as she had done. His common sense told him that on this account, too, he really had nothing with which to reproach himself. If he had persisted with his invitation, it was more likely that she would have told him not to bother to take her to the show. Common sense told him all the right things and Linus knew they were true, but Helen was dead and in somewhat bizarre circumstances, which suggested that maybe her death had not been necessary. Someone, therefore, should have been able to stop it. Linus's fear was that he might have been the one with that power. He reminded himself that Detective-Inspector Netley had indicated some small doubt about the identity of the corpse and Linus clung to this small uncertainty.

He was obliged to let go of it next day when Inspector Lacock turned up at Government Buildings and confirmed his colleague's opinion.

'Definitely an overdose,' he said. 'Heroin.

Did you have any idea she might have been on drugs?'

Linus shook his head. 'None at all. Mind you, I suppose that's not particularly significant: after all, if you're at the beginning of a relationship, you're likely to be a bit chary of confessing to being a junkie, don't you think?'

'She certainly wasn't a registered addict and her own doctor thinks it was most unlikely. What's more, we know there are no signs that she normally injected. There was just the one puncture mark.'

'Doesn't that tend to point to its being administered by someone else?'

'It makes that a strong possibility.' The policeman paused. 'We're wondering if there's a connection with Wingfield's death.'

'I thought that was straightforward heart failure?'

'It was. It's the bizarre situation of both corpses that makes us wonder, and both of them had received threats relating to the trial.'

'Are you no further forward with that?' Linus asked.

Lacock hesitated. 'Not really. This link—if that's what it proves to be—may give us the lead we've been searching for.'

'I can understand someone with a grudge going for the judge,' Linus remarked. 'I can understand their going for the jurymen or some of the more crucial witnesses, but Helen was just a lab technician doing her job. She had no other involvement than that. I can't see why she should be on the top of what would appear to be some sort of hit-list.'

'It does seem odd,' Lacock agreed. 'It may have been because she was available: the more obvious candidates were being discreetly watched. I don't think it crossed anyone's mind that a lab technician was in any danger.'

'Your watching seems to have been too discreet to save the judge,' Linus pointed out unkindly.

'We've been watching them since his death,' Lacock admitted. 'Threats are an everyday occurrence to judges. They almost never come to anything but we always have a slightly more acute surveillance of their homes on a permanent basis: the local beat-bobby keeps an eye on things.'

'By which you mean he slows down his panda car when he passes a judge's house, I take it?'

The Inspector was not amused. He changed the subject. 'Any idea what we should do about those funny little dogs? I don't suppose you'd like to take them on?'

'With Ishmael? How long do you think they'd last? What's happening to them at the moment?'

'The woman who was dog-sitting has come in to feed them, but she's made it clear she's not prepared to go on doing that indefinitely.'

'You can't blame her for that. Take them over to Thelwall. It won't cost much to feed them and it would be a pity to put them down. That would give us a chance to find any relatives or, failing that, some good homes for them.'

Lacock seemed surprised. 'There's two or three other people in that village with the same sort of dogs. Wouldn't it be more sensible to let them have them?'

'I don't think Helen would have been wild about that idea. No, let me have a word with young Thelwall.'

Linus sensed that the Thelwalls were not entirely overjoyed at the prospect of suddenly acquiring a number of dogs for an unspecified length of time but they fully appreciated Linus's reasons for not taking them home with him and, since he was happy to pay the food bills and the dogs need only occupy one kennel, they agreed to do so.

'We'll expect a return favour some day,' Ruth told him, only half jokingly.

'As long as it's legal, you'll get it,' Linus replied. 'With any luck it will only be for a few days, until they trace Helen's family. She must have some relatives, somewhere.'

The phone rang next morning as Linus was about to leave the house. He almost didn't pick it up but he was a neat-minded man and a telephone deliberately unanswered was an offence in his eyes almost comparable to a cluttered draining-board. He picked it up, glancing at his watch as he did so.

'Mr Rintoul?' said a woman's vaguely familiar voice. 'I don't suppose you remember me. We met at Windsor. Morwenna Leyburn—Amazonian Vampire Dogs.' The voice was authoritative, throaty and immediately conjured up the bosomy, robed figure of a no-longer-youthful Cleopatra with a heavy ankh nestling in her cleavage.

Linus remembered the little band of admiring cohorts and decided against pandering to her vanity. Her words might suggest self-deprecation. Her tone implied the reverse. Morwenna Leyburn would not be able to conceive the possibility that, once met, she was unforgettable.

'Leyburn, Leyburn,' Linus said in the somewhat absent tones of one casting around in his mind for the spark of familiarity. 'Weren't you the woman who went Best of Breed?'

The answering voice was carefully controlled, or so it seemed to Linus. 'Got it in one,' she said with forced pleasure. 'I'm ringing you at the suggestion of young Thelwall—the vet at Enstone that keeps the quarantine kennel.'

'I know who you mean,' Linus said.

'I've only just heard the tragic, tragic, news about poor Helen. Such a sweet girl. You were very friendly, I believe.'

'We knew each other quite well,' Linus admitted cautiously. He didn't like voices that dripped with honey, and particularly not ersatz honey.

'So sad. She had so much to offer the breed, but still, we just have to pick up the pieces and carry on, don't we?'

Linus was unsure what pieces relevant to Morwenna Leyburn there might be to pick up, so he said nothing. Let her find her own way of broaching whatever it was she had rung him for. He looked at his watch again. He could only be late now.

'As soon as I heard, I got on to the police,' she went on. 'I told them I'd take the dogs but they said they'd already gone to Mr Thelwall and when I spoke to him he said the matter was all in your hands.'

'I suppose it is,' Linus agreed. 'We're waiting for the police to trace some relatives. When they do, it will be up to them to decide what happens.'

'Didn't you know? Poor Helen had no relatives.'

'No close ones, perhaps, but there may well be more distant ones. It would certainly be wrong not to try to trace them.'

'Oh yes, of course: I didn't mean to imply anything else, but we do have to think of the dogs' welfare, and I really don't think a kennels is the right place for them.'

'Is there anything wrong with Thelwall's place?' Linus asked. 'If you know anything to his detriment, it is fairly important—after all, he has a quarantine licence.'

'No, no. I didn't mean to imply . . . It's just that Vampire Dogs don't really do well in kennelled conditions. They're much better in the home.'

Linus didn't doubt the truth of her remarks. They applied to most small breeds, but he was conceding nothing to Morwenna Leyburn, who, he suspected, had motives other than pure altruism for offering to take Helen's dogs.

'You needn't worry, Mrs . . . Leyburn.' Linus deliberately made a slight pause to imply that he had to think to recall her name. 'I'll be keeping a very close eye on them and if I'm not entirely happy, they'll be removed.'

His caller tried a new tack. 'What do you expect will happen to them?' she asked.

'Who knows? I suppose there's an outside chance the relative—if one is found—will want to keep them.'

'And if not?'

'We'll have to find them good homes.'

'Now there you could have difficulties. There really isn't much demand for them. They're delightful little dogs, of course, but too small for most people—they're afraid of stepping on them. If, on the other hand, they had their papers, we could find them homes within the breed.'

Now we get to it, Linus thought. Aloud, he said, 'I'm sure their papers are in the cottage somewhere. Or were: the police will have taken them away, but they'll be returned eventually and I'll bear your comments in mind. Thank you, you've been most helpful.'

It was an unmistakably end-of-conversation remark and Morwenna leapt in before he could put the phone down.

'It's not quite that simple,' she said hastily. 'You have to be able to identify the dogs without a shadow of doubt, and I don't think you were quite that absorbed in them.'

Linus knew she was quite right but his voice oozed confidence. 'I don't think identifying them will prove an insuperable barrier,' he said. 'Now, if you don't mind, I do have to go to work: I was about to leave when you rang, so I hope you'll not think me rude if I hang up now.'

She apologized profusely and with a sincerity roughly comparable to Linus's expressed wish not to be thought rude.

He had his key in the ignition when a thought struck him. He looked at his watch and hesitated. He really was very late. Still, another ten minutes couldn't make that much difference, not now. He dashed back indoors and picked up the telephone.

'Is Inspector Lacock available?' he asked. 'Tell him it's Linus Rintoul—Ministry of Agriculture.' Lacock would know exactly who Linus Rintoul was, but mention of a government department tended to have an expeditious effect on switchboard operators. Linus was lucky. He caught Lacock just as that individual was about to leave the Station. 'Lacock,' he said, 'did you happen to remove any of Helen Glenbarr's papers from the cottage?'

'We took her files, certainly,' the policeman said cautiously. 'Why?'

'Did they include the dogs' papers?'

'If you mean pedigrees and things, yes. No interest to us, of course. We'll be returning them.'

'No, don't. Hang on to them for the time being, will you? At least until you've traced her relatives and can hand them over to them. I don't suppose you've had any luck with that yet?'

'Hardly. Her death interests us rather more at the moment. Why? What's all this about?'

'I'm not sure. I'm probably just being paranoid, but I'd like to feel those particular papers were in safe hands—at least for the time being. There is one other thing.'

'Yes?'

'When—if—you do trace any relatives, would you let Thelwall or me know first? After you've seen them, of course.'

'You'll have to know—you've got the dogs,' Lacock pointed out reasonably.

'I know that, but we do want to make sure those dogs go to good homes and not just places where they'll be used as breeding machines. I've a hunch that certain interested parties would be very keen to make the relatives an offer they wouldn't want to refuse and I'd rather they didn't get it in before Thelwall or I have had a chance to talk to them.'

'If I didn't know you better, I'd suspect your own motives,' Lacock commented. 'You've nothing to worry about. Mrs Glenbarr will have left a sizeable estate when the value of the cottage is taken into account. We won't be giving out any information except to those who have a need to know. Will that satisfy you?'

It did, and Linus went to work in a considerably lightened state of mind.

* * *

It was a couple of days before he was able to go over to Enstone and look at Helen's dogs, though he had given Ruth the gist of his conversation with Lacock. When he reached the kennels he was very glad he had taken this precaution. He didn't recognize any of the handful of cars parked outside the surgery, except those belonging to Thelwall and his wife, but he did recognize the voice which penetrated the chipboard wall dividing the little waiting room from the surgery itself. Morwenna Leyburn's vocal cords certainly had a carrying quality about them.

Linus hesitated at the door, knowing that Thelwall would not take it amiss if he went straight in, but the conversation was too interesting to interrupt, so he took a seat with the rest of the small but engrossed audience and listened.

'...make sure he knows,' Morwenna was saying as he sat down.

'I'll certainly pass on your views,' Thelwall replied.

'I'd like to feel you were putting it a bit more strongly than that,' she went on. 'In any case, I can't quite see why you have to involve him at all. After all, the dogs are living here with you. It's you and your wife who have all the hard work. Quite an imposition when one starts to think about it. All you have to do is tell him you've considered the matter very carefully and decided they'd be better off with me.'

'Are you implying that this kennel doesn't look after its occupants adequately?'

'Goodness me, no! But you have to admit there's no comparison between caring for some great galumphing Labrador and caring for anything as small and delicate as a Vampire Dog.'

'I think I can cope.'

'I'm sure you can *cope*, Mr Thelwall, but I can offer a great deal more than just coping.'

'Then I'm afraid you will just have to offer it later, when we know what Mrs Glenbarr's relatives want to do about them,' Thelwall told her.

'They've traced some, have they?' Linus was aware of the sharpened interest.

'I don't think I said that. I certainly didn't mean to imply it. I find it hard to believe they won't find some relations sooner or later.'

'You will find they won't,' she said dogmatically. 'I was very friendly with poor Helen and I do know there were none.'

'We'll cross that bridge when we come to it,' Thelwall said. 'Now, if you don't mind, Mrs Leyburn, I do have patients waiting outside.'

'Very well, but I warn you, Mr Thelwall, if those dogs are put in the wrong homes, I'll make quite sure the Kennel Club doesn't allow any transfers. They'll be quite valueless.'

'I'll bear that in mind,' Thelwall said, opening the surgery door and ushering his caller out to the interested scrutiny of those waiting, one of whom was apparently not so interested, since he was studying a poster of the various breeds of cat and had his back to the surgery door at that moment.

Linus turned as Morwenna Leyburn's footsteps died away. 'I'll see you up at the house when you've finished,' he said.

'Fine. Ruth will give you some tea.'

While he waited for surgery to finish, Linus drank his tea and thumbed through the register of veterinary surgeons to locate John Chilson's address, which he then jotted down in the back of his diary.

David Thelwall didn't have much to add to what Linus had already overheard and from which he had deduced much that had gone before. It seemed that Mrs Leyburn's initial approach to the younger vet had been very much that of Lady Bountiful, anxious to relieve the lesser orders of some of their burdens, and when he had not jumped at the opportunity of being relieved of his responsibilities, she had begun to castigate Linus who, she said, took too much upon himself.

'She has a point,' Ruth commented. 'You are rather inclined to take other people's problems and try to solve them, and this one isn't even someone else's problem—it's the police's, and they do their own solving.'

'Do you want me to take the dogs away?' Linus asked. 'I will if they're really that much of a nuisance. I'll go to some lengths to stop that woman getting her hands on them, though: she's not bothered about their welfare. She wants the bloodlines and sees a way of getting it for free. Besides, she's just about the last person Helen would have wanted to see them end up with.'

'They're fine here,' David said. 'I don't like other people trying to push me around or manipulate me, and that's exactly what that woman was trying to do, and I'd like to see her fail to get them just out of sheer bloody-mindedness.'

That evening, Linus rang John Chilson. He reckoned that a colleague who knew the workings of the dog-game from the inside would be a better bet for giving him the information he wanted than some young office girl, however well-informed and helpful, simply because the girl, to whom he would be a complete stranger, would only be able to advise him by the rule book. Chilson might be more inclined to mention the greyer areas that bureaucracy always contains but prefers to disguise.

'If someone dies very suddenly, leaving a number of rather nice pedigree dogs,' Linus asked him, 'can they be given homes where they can still be shown?'

'Tricky,' Chilson admitted. 'If the owner had entered them for shows before he died, then they can compete in those, but they can't be entered in any others unless they've been transferred officially to the new owner's possession, and a transfer requires the signature of the previous owner.'

'Difficult, if that person's dead,' Linus

remarked.

'Very. I suppose the dogs would become the property of the heir and I imagine the KC would take the will as being adequate proof of a wish to transfer ownership. If I'm right, the heir would show them after applying to the KC, and once they were in his name, he could transfer them in the normal way to anyone else.'

'And what if there were no heir—or no will?'

'Very untidy. The simple answer is, I haven't a clue. I suppose whoever had taken charge of them would have to apply for special consideration but I can see one snag immediately.'

'What's that?'

'Somehow the KC would have to be satisfied that the person making the application knew beyond a shadow of a doubt which dog was which.'

'And how would that be proved?'

Chilson thought about that one for so long that Linus began to wonder whether the line had gone dead. Finally he said, 'There are two possibilities that I can think of. One would be for the dogs to be examined by an expert in the breed—a breed specialist who had seen the dogs at shows several times. It wouldn't be any use if they'd never been exhibited.'

'Let's assume they have been.'

'Right, then that would be one way. Not infallible, but it might be acceptable. A lot would depend on the KC's estimation of the integrity of the person doing the identifying.'

'The other way?'

'That would depend upon just how well organized the deceased owner was. If he kept detailed records and especially if there were photographs of the dogs with the dogs properly identified on the back, then I imagine those could be used.'

'What do you mean by "properly identified"?'

'A doggy-woggy blurred snapshot labelled 'Mopsy' wouldn't do. A professional photo with the dog's registered name on the back and, better still, its registration number, would. If it were a professional photo taken by one of the established canine photographers, that would be even better, because his files would identify the dog's benching number and the show at which the photo was taken, and from those details it would be easy to identify the dog, either as a back-up to anything written on the photo or instead. That would be particularly useful in a breed that can't be identified by markings. Labradors or Giant Schnauzers, for instance. Is all this any help?'

'Yes, very. There's one last point. From what you say, it would seem that the Kennel Club's discretion would be very important?'

'Absolutely crucial.'

'So a lot would depend upon the person

applying. An unknown Joe Bloggs would be less successful than a well-known exhibitor.'

'It would depend on what the exhibitor was well-known for. Some are pretty notorious, but in general I'd say, yes. Joe Bloggs might have to work harder for the same result. Can I ask a question?'

'Of course.'

'This wouldn't have anything to do with Helen Glenbarr's dogs, I suppose?'

'You suppose correctly.'

'Then the person to identify the dogs is that dreadful Leyburn woman. I don't like her and I don't think many people outside the breed do, but there's no denying she'd know the dogs.'

'All the same, I'd be obliged if you'd not mention this conversation to her—or to anyone else.'

'No problem—consider it forgotten.'

Linus replaced the receiver thoughtfully. Chilson had given him quite a lot to think about. It began to look as if Morwenna Leyburn had such a stranglehold on the world of Vampire Dogs that there was a very strong possibility her cooperation would be needed if the dogs were not to disappear into loving pet homes—not that Linus despised such homes, quite the contrary, but he knew that that was the last thing Helen would have wanted. She would have wanted them to be loved, yes, but she would also have wanted them to play their part in safeguarding the breed. It did not seem very probable that Morwenna would identify them unless it was in her interest to do so. Linus's far-off days in general practice had introduced him to more than one breeder who built up her breeding stock on the cheap by taking in 'rescue' cases. Helen would not have wanted that to happen with her dogs.

His old college chum might have given Linus something to think about, but it wasn't proving a very productive line of thought, mainly because Linus had no very clear idea what end result he had in mind. After all, provided the dogs were likely to be well looked after, what did it matter where they went? Helen would undoubtedly have had preferences, but Helen was dead. The dogs weren't and their interests must come first and Linus, as a vet, knew better than most that it wasn't necessarily easy to find good homes for adult dogs, even—or perhaps particularly—such tiny ones as these. He teased the question around while he drank his bedtime cocoa and was no further forward by the time he filled his empty cup with water and stood it methodically on the draining-board before he cast a glance round the kitchen prior to turning off the light and then did the same thing in the sitting-room. He had been brought up to be neat, tidy and methodical and sometimes envied those who were none of those things, but so deeply ingrained was his early training that the furthest he ever succeeded in going against it was to leave his shoes unpolished for the occasional night.

Clarification of his motives struck him at the top of the landing. One of his greatest treasures hung here: a Dulac illustration to *The Sleeping Beauty* which he had discovered in the days before the artist was collected and had bought, if not for the proverbial song, at least for a figure which had not broken the bank of a government vet—well, not by very much. It showed the guests returning to the castle after the christening of the Princess Aurora, depicting them, unusually, from the rear. It was a picture which always gave him a little frisson of pleasure whenever he came upstairs, partly on its own account and partly because there was no denying the satisfaction of having recognized the quality of an artist's work before he had been generally reinstated. Seeing it now brought suddenly to mind another in *The Sleeping Beauty* sequence, one for which Linus had no hankering. It showed the Fairy Uglyane cursing the shrouded royal cradle while the guests looked on aghast. The old crone was wreaking revenge for the slight of not having been invited to the ceremony, and Linus realized with some disgust that his motives in relation to Helen's dogs were closer to revenge than humanitarianism.

The revenge was against Morwenna

Leyburn, though it was hard to work out what the revenge was for, since, looked at dispassionately, all the woman had done was to express a willingness to take the dogs. It had something to do with the fact that that willingness had been accompanied by an implied threat of non-cooperation if her offer wasn't accepted and there was the recollection that she had done nothing to make Helen feel welcome; besides, there was something about her which made his flesh creep. These were poor excuses for 'revenge', about as feeble as the old excuse of the evil eye, and Linus was ashamed of himself for feelings which should not cross the mind of any civilized man. Nevertheless, those were his precise feelings in the matter and he slept all the better for having analysed them.

His brain must have gone on wrestling with the situation while he was asleep because when he woke up, he knew exactly what to do.

He telephoned Inspector Lacock. 'I suppose the police went through all Helen's papers?' he asked.

'Bound to, but Netley would know more about that than I do. Why?'

'I want to find out what shows those dogs are entered for,' Linus told him. 'I'll hazard a guess she's written it down somewhere, either on schedules or in some sort of record book.'

'What have you in mind?' The policeman's

tone was wary.

'If they were entered while she was alive, someone can exhibit them for her. I thought it might make it easier to find good homes for them,' he added untruthfully.

'I believe there were some kennel records,' Lacock conceded. 'I think they'll have been handed over to her relative, though: they had no bearing on her death, you see. We're sure it's connected with the death of Mr Justice Wingfield.'

'You traced someone, then?'

'Someone very remote, I believe. A second cousin who wasn't even aware of Mrs Glenbarr's existence. Netley had a word with her yesterday and I know he was going to give her anything that wasn't relevant to the case.'

'Presumably he asked her what she wanted to do about the dogs?'

'I imagine so, but I've not had a chance to speak to him. He'll get in touch with you eventually, I expect.'

Linus swore quietly and methodically to himself as he replaced the receiver. Then he tried to get hold of Detective-Inspector Netley and had to be content with leaving a message for him.

Somewhat to his surprise—because he didn't much like the man and was therefore disinclined to anticipate creditable behaviour from him—the detective contacted him that evening, just before Linus left Government Buildings. 'Sorry you had to ring,' he began. 'I'd have been in touch sooner but I had to fill in some paperwork. We've traced a relative of Mrs Glenbarr's, but she seems to be the only one. She didn't know your friend, so she was understandably not too upset. Mind you, she wasn't displeased to learn she'd inherited everything, though she managed to disguise it quite well. I asked her about the dogs and she's not interested. She just said, "Put them down." She's the sort who plumps up cushions behind you and would empty an ashtray every time a bit of ash fell in it—if she allowed smoking, which she almost certainly doesn't. A dog in that house would be disastrous.'

'Nothing about finding good homes?' Linus said, dismayed.

'Said she couldn't be bothered. I have to confess I didn't press the matter.'

'Is there any reason why I shouldn't?' Linus asked.

'None at all, since you're paying for their keep just now. I don't think she cares much what happens to them. I'd hazard a guess that she'll jump at the chance of being relieved of them.'

'Lacock says he thinks you handed over to her Helen's kennel records. Do you think she'd let me have them?'

'I don't see why not. They'll be no use to her.

Her name's Mrs Muckross—Edna Muckross. Lives in Neasden.'

Linus rang her immediately, loath to run the risk, now that she had been traced, of Morwenna Leyburn's getting there first. From the little Netley had said, it sounded as if she would take the best offer she could, so he needed to get in first, before she discovered that there might be another one. He was tempted to ask Netley not to pass on the details to anyone else, but suspected that that might place the policeman in a difficult position where professional ethics were concerned.

Mrs Muckross's tone was frosty, her words guarded. The police had already discussed with her the future of Helen Glenbarr's dogs. Her decision had been made, and that was all there was to it. Dogs were nasty, messy things; she wasn't having them in her own house and only a woolly-minded sentimentalist would want to persuade her to change her mind.

'I'm a vet, Mrs Muckross,' Linus told her. 'I'm hardly a woolly-minded sentimentalist. I work for the Ministry of Agriculture.' This statement was totally irrelevant but Linus knew there was a certain type of person to whom any firm connection with a government department implied a respectable and unimaginative solidity. He rather thought Mrs Muckross might come into that category. 'May I visit you? I shan't take up much of your time. One afternoon, perhaps?'

* * *

Suburban houses don't have to be dull. This was one. Dull and respectable. The curtains in the bay window had been drawn almost completely across, not, Linus suspected, out of respect for a dead relative, but to prevent the feeble English sunshine fading the carpets and when Mrs Muckross opened the door, Linus found himself looking at the personification of her voice—tall, thin and grey. Her hair was dragged back in the sort of tight bun that he hadn't seen since he was at school and her clothes had that shapeless, knitted look of a certain type of post-First World War spinster aunt. The title 'Mrs' seemed so inapplicable that he wondered whether she had adopted it much as housekeepers used to do, as a symbol of office rather than a legal fact.

He followed her down the long, thin passage, noting the spotless linen drugget that covered the stair-carpet, fastened in place by gleaming brass rods. She showed him into what Linus would have called the dining-room and she probably referred to as the back parlour. The furniture was firmly from the 'thirties, wooden, bulbous and the recipient of fifty years of conscientious polishing; the fireplace of stepped fawn tiles, the 'autumn tints' carpet (all those leaves so good at not showing the dirt) were equally evocative of their period, and an erect and rigid armchair beside the fireplace betrayed the fact that this was where Mrs Muckross spent most of her time. That is to say, Linus amended to himself, the time when she isn't polishing something.

To open the conversation, he said, 'Have you lived here long, Mrs Muckross?'

She looked surprised, whether at his impertinence or his interest he wasn't quite sure. 'Since it was built. My late husband and I moved in when we came back from our honeymoon. Would you like a cup of tea?'

Linus said he would and tried to imagine Mrs Muckross having a honeymoon. It wasn't easy.

The tray, he decided, had probably been a wedding-present, the lazy-daisy traycloth had almost certainly been embroidered by his hostess and he wasn't the least bit surprised that the tea-service was of bone china, and matched. No assorted supermarket mugs in this household. She handed him a plate of chocolate digestives. 'Take a plate,' she told him. 'You won't want to balance it on your saucer.'

Linus did as he was told. There were, he noticed, no dog-hairs in the tea, a fact which set this house apart from his own, the Thelwalls' and Helen's, to say nothing of most of those he visited professionally. This was indeed no place for a dog, not even a small one.

'I don't want to take up a lot of your time, Mrs Muckross,' he began. 'Helen's dogs are at present being looked after at a kennels belonging to a colleague of mine but at my expense. I was a friend of Helen's,' he added since such altruism as he might be thought to be claiming was likely to be regarded with some suspicion by someone like Mrs Muckross. 'There are two things I'd like from you, the second dependent upon the first. I'd like your permission to keep the dogs alive and try to find good homes for them eventually.'

'Why don't you keep them yourself?'

'I already have a dog and he isn't particularly charitably disposed towards others of his kind. Helen's tiny things wouldn't last five minutes.'

'Hmm. That sounds honest enough. How much do you intend to make out of them?'

'For what it's worth, that's not my intention. I hope that I can find them good homes within the breed, where I gather their bloodlines will be useful. I don't believe in giving dogs away as a general rule—it's my professional observation that people don't value dogs they get as a gift. I want to take them to the shows that Helen has already entered them for and I hope to recoup some of the costs I've incurred in paying for their keep and so on. Does that seem reasonable?'

'Eminently—put like that. I gather it's quite a rare breed. Once you've got my permission, you could make quite a good thing out of it.'

Mrs Muckross's house might be pure 'thirties, but her mind was well up to date.

'I might. I'm not sure. You'll just have to take my word for it that that isn't my intention.'

Mrs Muckross studied him with some astuteness. 'And what was the second thing?' she asked.

'If you agree to let me have the dogs, I shall need Helen's kennel records which I understand the police have handed over to you. These will include pedigrees and registration certificates which will be needed for new owners. There should also be show schedules which will tell me which dogs are entered for which shows, and I hope there will also be some photographs.'

'Which you will need to be able to distinguish one dog from another, I presume,' Mrs Muckross finished for him.

'Precisely,' Linus agreed. There were no flies on Mrs Muckross.

She rose and went over to a small oak bureau and pulled out one of its drawers which she then placed upon the table before him.

'Everything the police gave me is in here,' she said. 'Sort through it and take out what you need.'

She refilled his teacup and put the plate of biscuits beside it on the table before taking the tray out into the kitchen. She had obviously decided to trust him.

Helen had been meticulously well organized, Linus now discovered. All the kennel papers were here, marshalled in a systematic order, a filing-envelope each for pedigrees, registration papers, inoculation certificates, show and breeding records for each dog—and those essential professional photographs. The only item among the dog papers that did not seem immediately relevant was a red leather-bound notebook of the sort sold with blank pages to aspiring journal-keepers. The fly-leaf said simply 'Dog Diary', and Linus hesitated. One did not read other people's diaries. Still, it might be important, so he flicked over the pages, but it seemed to contain nothing but notes on food, on grooming techniques and, more crucially from Linus's point of view, references to visits to the vet. These, however, were soon proved to be reported in greater detail in the veterinary record of each dog so, given Linus's natural distaste for delving into someone's private diary, however innocuous its contents might appear, he excluded that from the papers he decided to take and drew Mrs Muckross's attention to the fact that he had.

She nodded approvingly. 'I thought you'd leave that,' she said. 'I left it in just to see if I was right. When you want any signatures from me, get in touch.' She hesitated and when she spoke again she sounded almost apologetic.

'You must think it strange that I'm not at all upset over this business,' she said. 'I don't think I ever met Helen Glenbarr, not even as a child. Her mother and I were cousins but we lost touch even before we had left school. It was never what you might call a close family. I'm afraid Helen meant no more to me than a total stranger would. You do understand?'

CHAPTER SIX

Ruth roared with laughter when Linus went along to the kennels armed with Helen's records and announced his intention of showing her dogs.

'This I shall have to see,' she announced, wiping the tears from her eyes. 'Linus, I don't think the show world is at all your scene. I can just about imagine you showing something like Ishmael, but I really can't envisage you poncing round with one of these tinies on the end of a bit of string. Or will you get yourself a Demis Roussos caftan and some beads and do it in the Long Blessington style?' The image this conjured up struck her as so hilariously funny that she had to support herself against the worktop while she found another tissue.

Linus glanced at her husband and saw that he, too, was indulging in a far from respectful grin. 'She's right, Linus,' he said. 'Your battle scars don't look out of place with Ishmael on the end of the lead but those Vampire Dogs are something else.'

Linus was disconcerted and instinctively fingered the neatly trimmed beard that, he had always believed, hid the worst of his scars. 'Do they show that much?' he asked.

Ruth shot a warning glance at her husband before speaking. 'No, they don't,' she said positively. 'But they're not completely hidden, either. You must know that. I doubt if most people even notice, but they do give you a rather macho look which doesn't quite fit with such dainty little dogs. Mind you,' she added reassuringly, 'it would look even more incongruous with a Toy Poodle on the end of the lead.'

Thanks in part to the dogs' markings and in part to Helen's photos, they were able without much difficulty to sort out which dog was which and then identify those which were due to be exhibited in the near future. Then, amid renewed hilarity, Linus took each dog in turn on one of the long, thin show leads which did indeed look like a piece of string but were actually made of nylon and were deceptively strong. Thus equipped, he went out on to the patch of grass behind the bungalow and tried to remember what he had seen the exhibitors do in the ring.

He realized straight away that he had not been as observant as he thought. It didn't seem to matter whether he kept the lead loose or taut, or whether he kept the dog close to his side or at arm's length, nor did it make much difference which dog was on the end of the lead. Without exception they either leapt up and down like animated yo-yos or spun round and round like whirligigs. One did both. It was a far cry from the carefully controlled, evenly paced, steady trot up and down that he had watched the dogs execute in the ring. It had looked remarkably easy and he knew he couldn't even blame it on lack of training: these dogs were seasoned show dogs: they had been trained by Helen. The trouble was, they knew he hadn't.

'You're wasting your time,' Ruth told him at last. 'I know what you need. Put the dogs away and come indoors. I'll see what I can drum up.'

Linus did as he was told, assuming she would have a good stiff drink ready for him. Instead, he found her in the middle of a telephone call.

'. . . so we can slot in three a week if he doesn't mind travelling?' she was asking as he came in. She glanced up at him and waved him over to the kettle and the jar of coffee, putting a hand over the mouthpiece. 'Make yourself some coffee,' she whispered. 'The kettle's just boiled.' Then she returned to her call. 'I'll tell him that. I'm sure he'll be there. Be gentle with him, Bet.' She replaced the receiver. 'I've found you a woman,' she announced.

'Oh, yes,' Linus said warily, guessing she might not mean the words in quite the way he was intended to interpret them. 'What would I want with one of them?'

'This one can be very useful to you. Do you know Bet Longwick?'

'Should I?'

'You might. You're a vet and she's got a small flock of fancy sheep. She also has gundogs and she runs ring-craft classes in various village halls in the evenings. She's a sensible, down-to-earth woman and she'll take you on if you want a sort of crash course and provided you don't mind three evenings a week in different villages.'

Linus hesitated. It had never crossed his mind he might be letting himself in for something like this. He'd had some vague idea that he'd pick the dogs up on a Saturday or Sunday morning, tootle along to wherever the show was and then tootle back again after their classes. This was beginning to look serious. 'Do I have to?' he said.

'No, of course you don't.' Ruth was obviously surprised. 'I thought the object was to find homes for the dogs among breeders and it's at dog shows where you'll find them. There doesn't seem much point in going to dog shows with them if you're not out to win. I know I don't know much about this game but I'm willing to bet you're not going to do much winning unless the dogs go better for you than they are at present.'

Linus reckoned her bet was a safe one but he instinctively covered his rear. 'Whatever happened to the Olympic spirit?' he asked defensively.

'You mean it's taking part that counts, and all that? Rubbish. It's winning that counts—and I suspect it always has been.'

Linus, whose view of human nature was as cynical as the next man's, made no attempt to dispute it.

* * *

Bet Longwick was middle-aged with a hockey-player's calves, cropped, iron-grey hair and a nice line in badge-embellished quilted jackets in that useful shade of vomit-green so favoured by country-dwellers. She was also everything Ruth had said she was. Linus found her terrifying.

She had an undoubted knack when it came to handling dogs. An animal that was a whirling dervish in Linus's hands moved up and down for Bet Longwick with an invisible halo over its head and butter in its mouth. By the end of the third class Linus, too, had stopped his charges from spinning like tops and they only did their yo-yo imitations some of the time. If he marvelled at Bet's dog-handling ability, he was only slightly less impressed at her patience with his own ineptitude but when he said as much, she looked surprised.

'You're really quite good. You should see some of the morons I get. At least I only have to tell you something once.'

Linus couldn't remember a more gratifying compliment, a fact which, he thought afterwards, either said something about him or about Bet Longwick. He wasn't sure which.

* * *

On the morning of the first show, he woke up feeling distinctly queasy. He rarely felt ill and cast his mind over the previous day's meals in an effort to account for it. There was nothing obvious. After the third trip to the loo he began to think that he was going to have to cry off the show. The fact that his stomach would settle down almost as soon as that decision was made was a clear indication that it wasn't food that was to blame, but nerves. He steeled them and went.

His appearance at the benches with Helen's dogs prompted comment and surprise. Marion Curbridge, who had, he vaguely remembered, agreed to keep an eye on the dogs while he and Helen had gone to find Chilson, was genuinely pleased to see them.

'I was so sorry to hear about Helen,' she said. 'The two of you seemed such good friends. Someone said it was suicide, which I must say came as a great surprise to me—I shouldn't have thought she was the type.'

'Neither would I,' Linus agreed, casting his mind back to consider whether anything that had appeared in the press might have given rise to the supposition of suicide. He couldn't remember anything, so perhaps it was just attributable to the grapevine.

'Still,' Mrs Curbridge went on, 'an overdose does rather point to that, doesn't it?'

Linus was quite sure that no mention of an overdose had appeared anywhere, but he supposed it was more than likely that police enquiries had extended to other AVD exhibitors and they might well have mentioned it—after all, they had raised the possibility when they spoke to him. 'So it might appear,' he conceded. 'The flaw in that conclusion, however, is the fact that there seems to be no suggestion that Helen ever took drugs of any sort. I hope the police can get to the bottom of it.'

'And if they don't?'

'Then it will be up to me, won't it?' He laughed. 'Perhaps I'd better start now. Can you throw any light on it?'

Mrs Curbridge, who appeared to take his comment entirely seriously, hastily disclaimed any knowledge of Helen's private habits. 'We only met at dog shows, you know. Still, I'm so glad her dogs aren't to be lost to us,' she said. 'Have you taken them over? Helen had agreed to let me use Munchkin on my Poppet. Will it still be possible, do you think?'

This was a query Linus hadn't anticipated and he knew it would be unfair to say 'yes' when there was every chance the dogs would be somewhere else when the appropriate time came. On the other hand, he was very much aware of Morwenna Leyburn's prehensile ears reaching out in his direction to catch any part of the conversation they could, and it was no part of his plan to let her know that other homes would eventually be sought for the dogs in question.

'I don't see why not,' he hedged. 'To tell the truth, I'm very new to all this and that's something I haven't so far given any thought to at all. You're not in a desperate rush, I hope?'

'Goodness me, no. Poppet won't be in season for another four months or so. I expect you'll know where you stand by then, won't you?'

'I certainly hope so,' he replied and they both laughed.

Morwenna Leyburn picked her time more carefully before making her own comment and did so when that section of the benches was temporarily empty of exhibitors. Her smile was as wide and as indefinably patronizing as ever, provoking in Linus a reprehensible desire to smack it from her face. He busied himself with the dogs instead.

'I hadn't realized you were so smitten with our little Vampires,' she said with a winsomeness more fitting to a ten-year-old.

'No reason why you should have,' he said. He thought that covered it rather well and hoped a calculated curtness would send her away. He had reckoned without the armadillo-hide of the average dog-exhibitor on the scent.

'And to be sure which dog is which, too! You realize, of course, that if you guess wrongly, there's bound to be some disgruntled competitor who will slap down their £25 and Kennel-Club you.'

Linus's experience of dog shows was far too recent and restricted for him to have encountered these particular phrases but he was astute enough to guess their inference—and a good enough judge of human nature to guess that the queue of disgruntled competitors was likely to be headed by Mrs Leyburn.

He smiled reassuringly. 'I don't think you'll find much guesswork comes into it. I know which dog is which.'

Her eyes narrowed but the smile, if anything, grew wider. Linus thought it was beginning to look forced. 'I'm glad of that,' she said. 'I did think it would be left to me to identify them.'

'We didn't want to impose on your good nature,' Linus lied, smiling in his turn, and had the pleasure of seeing her smile fade as she tried to work out for herself just how he could be so sure there would prove to be no mistakes of identification.

Linus, listening to comment at the ringside and around the benches, learned that the judge was an 'all-rounder' which seemed to mean that he was prepared to judge almost any breed. This, Linus decided, contemplating the vast variation between the different breeds, must mean that he was either extremely knowledgeable or extremely conceited. One's opinion on which category he came into probably depended upon how well one's dogs did under his judgement.

There were seven Vampire Dogs in Munchkin's class and Linus, whose stomach as he stood at the ringside waiting for the previous one to finish felt as if it were churning butter, was relieved to find that his nerves dropped away once he was in the ring. He collected his ring number and fastened it into the clip that had fortunately been among Helen's kennel paraphernalia. Then, remembering Bet Longwick's advice, he positioned himself roughly half way along the line of exhibitors.

To his relief, Munchkin—whose *alter ego* was a whirling, leaping demon—behaved as perfectly as Linus could have wished, well aware, or so it seemed to his inexperienced handler, of the difference between the show-ring, where one worked, and the training-class or garden, where one didn't. He stood like a rock on the table, ears erect, tail tightly curled, while the judge examined him in detail and then, on the floor, gave one thorough shake and trotted happily along, neither too close to Linus nor too far from him on a lead that was neither taut nor unduly slack, first in the required triangle and then up and down. That completed, he stood alertly gazing at his handler while the judge had a last all-round look at him and then, back in his place in the line, he continued to stand in that faultless pose while the remaining dogs were seen.

This is too good to last, Linus thought. Any moment now he's going to blow it. He wasted no time flattering himself that his handling had anything to do with the dog's performance. Munchkin knew exactly what he was doing.

So hard was Linus concentrating on his dog, willing him not to relax, that the judge had to call him twice and then touch him on the arm to bring him into the centre of the ring to stand in what Linus thought and everyone else knew, to be first place. Linus recognized the handler who stood below him. It was the man who had judged in place of Mr Justice Wingfield. Linus had seem him round the benches and checked in the catalogue, so he knew that the dog in second place had been bred by Morwenna Leyburn. Those further down the line he scarcely noticed and certainly did not identify. The steward handed out the prize-cards and rosettes, calling out the exhibits' numbers as he did so. The red awards for first place were greeted by a little—a very little—polite clapping. The blue ones for second provoked a storm of applause, both clapping and shouting. Linus had never before heard a claque in action and now that he had, and had been the object of its attentions, he liked it even less than he would have expected to. He hadn't expected it at all, of course. No one had even hinted at the possibility. There had been Ruth's cynical comment about the importance of winning, but he didn't think she had meant anything like this. His pleasure in a win—a win which the dog's behaviour alone might have entitled him to—had been destroyed.

Munchkin had won Open Dog and was therefore challenged by any unbeaten dogs for Best Dog, the winner of which would challenge the Best Bitch for Best of Breed. Linus had no idea of the relative merits of Helen's dog against the winner of the Junior and Post-Graduate classes. They certainly didn't show as well as Munchkin and he wondered whether the judge's nerve had failed him when Best Dog was given to Mrs Leyburn's Junior winner, Helen's dog taking the Reserve card. He nerved himself to smile and congratulate her but it cost him dear, particularly when the claque burst out into uninhibited cheering as he did so.

Back at the bench, Mrs Curbridge apologized embarrassedly for what had happened. 'I don't understand it,' she said. 'I'm sure they can't have realized how it looked. I do hope it won't put you off coming again.'

Linus smiled routinely and told her not to give it another thought as he certainly didn't intend to.

'Thank goodness,' she said. 'I think, if it had been me, I'd have wanted to curl up and die, but then, that's a woman for you,' and she giggled a little self-consciously.

Linus thought bitterly that she had summed it up rather well—and gender made very little difference. A desire to curl up and die figured fairly prominently in his own feelings right now, superseded, perhaps, by a more practicable desire to cut and run. However, when the bitch classes were over and everyone had returned to the benching tent, the curious glances thrown his way were the surest indication that his best ploy was to appear unmoved by the experience. He had never been much of a poker-player, but he thought he acquitted himself with a creditable degree of insouciance which he managed to sustain until three o'clock, when the rules permitted the removal of exhibits and his departure with the majority of exhibitors from all breeds could occasion no comment.

He succeeded in maintaining the outward appearance of indifference through the delighted exclamations of the Thelwalls at his success and the subsequent journey home. Then, when he sank down into an armchair with a cup of coffee, the reaction set in and he found himself trembling with a mixture of feelings, the component parts of which he analysed as being disgust, fear and pure anger. There had been no hint of a claque at Windsor, but then, given the identity of the substitute judge, there had been no need for one. More relevant, perhaps, was the fact that Helen had never referred to one. It might have been because she found it too disgusting to admit to and that, Linus thought, was entirely possible: he himself felt almost as if he had been sat upon and had not felt inclined to mention it to the Thelwalls. On the other hand, it might never have happened to Helen, and then again, it might have in her early days, but, by sticking it out, the perpetrators had finally given up. He revised his third scenario almost as soon as it occurred to him. Helen had moved to Long Blessington in the hope that living in closer proximity to other AVD breeders might lead to more friendly relationships between them. Relationships prior to her move had therefore by definition not been friendly, but he found it hard to imagine that anything remotely resembling what he had experienced that day would have allowed her to delude herself that things might improve.

Munchkin—a name, if ever there was one, chosen by a woman—had another show next weekend. Linus shuddered. It was a prospect that appealed so little that he rather thought he might develop a handy twenty-four-hour bug for the occasion and as soon as that idea occurred to him, he felt the lightening of a burden lifted.

The sense of relief remained with him for at least thirty seconds, to be replaced with the sinking feeling that comes when one is offered an easy way out and knows one won't take it. Linus had set himself the task of both fulfilling Helen's ambitions for her dogs and of thwarting Morwenna Leyburn's plans to get them into her own possession or see them lost to the dog fancy. If he let an unpleasant incident keep him away from shows, she was winning because the upshot could only be the placing of the dogs eventually in pet homes where they might well be very happy but their bloodlines—and with them, all Helen's work—would be lost. He wasn't giving in that easily. No matter how much effort it cost him, he would be at next week's show.

He fished the schedule out of the pile and studied it. As ever, the judge's name meant nothing to him though a cross-reference to that day's catalogue suggested that it was not a current exhibitor. He decided it might be worthwhile to find out a little more and rang Bet Longwick. She knew the name, but not well.

'She'd call herself an all-rounder, I expect,' she said. 'She's fairly new on the judging scene; one of those people who'll tackle anything. She was probably sitting at the ringside today watching to see what faces were winning and I'll bet you anything you like, those are the faces that will win next week. You're probably wasting your time, but the experience will be useful.'

It was not the most encouraging of forecasts but at least it meant he had nothing to lose by going and quite a bit to gain: there was always the off-chance she might do the unexpected but, more importantly, if the claque had been organized to drive him away, he would have the satisfaction of demonstrating that it had failed.

It was all very well to bolster himself up during the week that followed with thoughts such as these but when he woke up on Sunday morning, it seemed as if the convenient twenty-four-hour bug really had struck. He forced it by sheer will-power into a state of semi-submission and his determination paid off because, by the time he reached the showground, the worst he had to contend with was a stomach that had contorted itself into knots that would have made the centre-fold spread in *The Lancet* if they could have been photographed.

At least Marion Curbridge seemed pleased to see him and he wondered why so demonstrably normal a woman had become involved in a breed which attracted so many bizarre followers.

'I did wonder whether you'd come,' she said, a shade apologetically.

'Why shouldn't I?' Linus replied. 'After all, the dogs have been entered. It would be a pity to waste the opportunity.' They were words which required some bravado but he was glad he made the effort because he found he felt better as soon as they were uttered.

Mrs Curbridge looked at him with a degree of admiration that was balm to his stomach, if not to his soul. 'Well, quite,' she said. 'We all have to stick together, don't we?'

The question was both rhetorical and revealing and, since it required no answer, Linus just smiled.

He had brought a bitch as well as Munchkin. Her pet name was Yum-Yum and Linus wondered irreverently whether Helen had had some sort of hang-up about food when it came to naming her dogs.

The robes-and-beads brigade seemed surprised to see him and less than entirely pleased. Morwenna was the most successful at hiding any displeasure she might have felt. She was attending to her dogs on their bench when he arrived and he noticed one of her disciples nudge her and nod in his direction. Morwenna straightened up and looked at him, flicking her Cleopatra-trimmed locks back from her round face. For the second time it crossed Linus's mind that the unnaturally even colour and the precisely symmetrical cut might actually be a wig. Her customary enveloping smile took a while to develop and not until it was securely in place did she greet him.

'Still waving the flag, I see. You must be really keen.'

Linus forced himself to smile blandly back. 'Some of Helen's enthusiasm seems to have rubbed off on me,' he told her.

'So it would appear. I gather you've got her kennel records as well. Quite a useful little bonus.'

Linus said neither yea nor nay but he did wonder how she knew. If it was more than an inspired shot in the dark, she must also know that a relative had been found—a relative with the power to sign over the dogs to a third party. He had a strong urge to press her and find out just how much she did know but, if she were guessing, to do so would be to reveal too much and if she were not, it might be better tactics to appear indifferent. He did, however, send up a small, silent prayer of gratitude that he had had the forethought to get to Mrs Muckross first. He must now place dependence upon her seeing through Morwenna Leyburn. Looking at that lady, he didn't think Mrs Muckross would have been greatly impressed but it was entirely possible that Mrs Leyburn did not always dress as she did for dog shows.

Morwenna made no further attempt at conversation but it wasn't long before the tall, thin hippy-reject whom the catalogue identified as Nick Fidden came across and paused by Linus's cage.

He studied the two dogs in silence. 'The dog's a bit off-colour, don't you think?' he said at last.

'Really? I hadn't noticed,' Linus said frostily.

'Well, you wouldn't, would you? I mean, you're new to all this.'

Linus looked at him icily. 'Funny sort of thing to say to a vet,' he remarked.

Fidden was unmoved. 'Oh, are you?' he said. 'I didn't know.'

Liar, Linus thought. The Leyburn woman certainly knew and he doubted very much that she hadn't passed the information on.

Fidden shifted to the other leg, his weight supported by the division between Linus's bench and the next one. 'Didn't think we'd see you again,' he volunteered.

'Which doesn't make you a very good judge

of character, does it?' Linus replied affably and had the satisfaction of seeing a flush spread over the emaciated cheeks. He hoped the man would go away, but he didn't.

'This won't be your day, you know,' Fidden went on.

'Probably not,' Linus agreed, refusing to be needled.

'This judge doesn't go for Helen's type and, in any case, she knows which side her bread's buttered.'

Linus fixed his gaze on the other man. 'Does that mean she's been bought?' he asked.

'No, no, I didn't mean that,' came the hasty disclaimer. 'It's just that she's an up-and-coming all-rounder who wants to get on the judging lists. It's my guess she'll go for the dogs whose owners have the power to put her there.'

'You're saying that she's dishonest,' Linus pointed out.

The man looked surprised. 'I don't call that dishonest,' he protested.

'Don't you? I suppose that explains your own judging.' Linus removed his attention from Nick Fidden and absorbed himself in his dogs. Fidden hovered indecisively for a few moments and then took himself off. His place was filled by Marion Curbridge.

'Oh, dear,' she said. 'That wasn't very wise. He's very annoyed.'

'Ah, but was it true?' Linus asked.

'That's why he was annoyed. I think you struck rather too close to the bone.'

Linus straightened up and looked at her. 'You seem a nice woman, Mrs Curbridge. Why do you carry on?'

'I like the dogs,' she said simply. 'It does get very unpleasant at times, especially when the "right" people don't win, but I keep my head down and battle on. I did hope, when Helen Glenbarr came along, that we'd at least find things a little better balanced, especially when she got a judging appointment. Now she was the sort of person who really would have judged the dogs and not the other end of the lead. Still, it wasn't to be.'

'Does your family share your interest?' he asked.

'My family?' Linus had the odd impression that he had somehow thrown her off-balance. 'Oh, you must mean my son. No. Well, I suppose he might but he's . . . away from home and I don't see much of him these days.'

'You must have found Helen quite a pleasant companion—the two of you being what I can only describe as islands of normality in this breed.'

She laughed self-consciously. 'I hadn't thought of it quite like that. It doesn't bother me too much, you know. I just do my own thing and they leave me alone. Sometimes I win—not very often, but sometimes—and they go through the motions of congratulating me. When I see how they treat some other people, I'm quite glad I'm not more successful.'

It was, Linus thought, one of the most damning appraisals of a situation that he had ever heard.

The judge proved to be not so shallow as he had been led to believe. Yum-Yum was placed in the lower cards of her class but Munchkin won Open Dog and went on to take Best Dog and Best of Breed. There was only a little polite clapping from one or two of the ring-siders, among them Mrs Curbridge, but there was at least no regeneration of that dreadful claque.

'You're new to the breed, aren't you?' the judge said to him afterwards. 'I thought you must be the one Mrs Leyburn was referring to on the phone the other day. I can't say I agree with her. I thought he was a delightful dog—and so sound.' She laughed a little self-consciously. 'I dare say she'll never speak to me again after today.'

Linus was tempted to tell her to count her blessings but he smiled politely instead. So Morwenna didn't rely entirely upon her face being known. He could imagine the technique: the phone call on some innocuous subject, the casual change of emphasis; the mention of a new exhibitor. Where would she take it from there? She was far too clever just to damn someone else's dog—no judge would interpret that as anything other than sour grapes. It would be far more effective to praise the dog in question and then to finish with something like, 'Yes, a lovely dog. *Such* a pity about . . .' in this case, Linus suspected, such a pity about his movement. Maybe something would be added about this fault being such a crucial one in the breed. The skill would lie in not laying it on too thickly, and then swiftly turning the conversation back into uncontentious matters before hanging up. That way Morwenna would appear in the judge's mind as the generous-minded competitor, happy to acknowledge the quality of someone else's dog, while effectively putting in a very subtle boot.

This was not, Linus decided, a very nice game.

CHAPTER SEVEN

Two days later a package arrived for Linus. His cleaning woman had taken it in and it was waiting for him on the worktop along with the electricity bill, a reminder that his NBRC subscription was due and a circular urging him to attend a sale of bankrupt oriental carpets.

The package was the size and shape of a shoe-box. There was no sender's address on it and the postmark was smudged. Linus studied all these carefully because, since it was nowhere near his birthday and he had no other anniversaries which might provoke presents, he had absolutely no idea at all what it might be or who might have sent it. He did wonder briefly about letter-bombs, but weren't they always in those padded envelopes? In any case, there was no reason why he should receive one of those, either.

All the same, he opened it with great care. First he untied the string instead of either cutting it or sliding it off one end. Then he slid a knife under the sticky-tape at each end and along the join. He spread the paper out and found it did indeed cover a shoe-box. He looked at the label. It depicted a man's very ordinary lace-up shoe of the sort worn by town-dwellers throughout the country and it carried the name of a well-known multiple shoe-shop. He sliced through the sticky tape that kept the lid in place. The box was full of tissue paper. Confident now that there were no suspicious wires—and telling himself he was being a fool to expect any—he removed the carefully crumpled tissue and slapped Ishmael, who had suddenly become most interested in what he was doing, on the muzzle. Then he discovered why the dog was so interested.

Lying on its bed of tissue was the body of an Amazonian Vampire Dog—and it was very,

very dead.

* * *

Accustomed as he was in his professional capacity to the bodies of dead animals, Linus nevertheless stepped back in revulsion. When an animal needed to be destroyed, for whatever reason, he got on and destroyed it without any strong feelings: it was, after all, his job. He had even fewer feelings about disposing of the subsequent carcase, being firmly of the opinion that what happened to the body once it had been humanely killed was unimportant, though, in the case of pet animals, the feelings of the owners had to be taken into concerned account. He felt much the same about his own death, being of the opinion that funerals were a waste of money. Their importance lay only in their way of helping the survivors come to terms with their grief. He hoped that no one would waste a funeral on him: his body could go for medical research and a memorial service, if that was felt necessary, which was in his opinion the most that would be required.

But there were forms of death with which he could not come to terms. Murder was one of them. Death through neglect, deliberate or otherwise, was another and, while the treatment meted out to the corpse could be of no importance to the body itself, sending it through the post to an unsuspecting recipient betrayed a mind so twisted as to verge on the deranged.

Besides, he couldn't be sure it wasn't one of Helen's dogs.

It was the right colour—a golden red and white—but that coloration was not exclusive to Helen's dogs. It is a phenomenon of those long-coated breeds whose fur in life customarily stands off from the skin beneath that in death, when blood is no longer flowing through the skin, the fur collapses, lying every which way and completely altering the appearance of the dog. The body is further distorted by rigor mortis, the side on which the animal lies in death becoming as flat and rigid as the proverbial board. A devoted owner would still recognize the dog. A stranger—and in this context Linus was a stranger—would not be sure. He went to the telephone.

'Hello, Ruth. Sorry to bother you with what will seem like a silly question, but are all the Vampire Dogs there?'

There was a pause while Ruth Thelwall tried to fathom the implications of the question. 'Yes,' she said. 'At least, they were when I went to feed them this evening. Why?'

'You're quite sure? I mean, you counted them? You couldn't have missed one?'

'No, Linus. I couldn't. I always count at feeding-time just to make sure every dog is eating and if one of them isn't, then David has a look at it to find out why. What's this all about?'

'Nothing,' Linus lied. 'Just something that crossed my mind. Silly, really. You'd let me know if anything happened to one of them, wouldn't you?'

'Of course I would!' Linus could tell she was offended. 'After all, you're paying their food bills, remember. Or do you think we're ripping you off?'

Since the thought had never crossed his mind, he was appalled at the suggestion. 'Good God, no, Ruth. Look, I'll explain it sometime but not now. It's a bit peculiar and if I hadn't been thrown off balance I'd have realized they must all be there still.' The postmark was smudged but it must have been posted at least the previous day, probably in the morning, and he should have realized that, had the Thelwalls found one of Helen's dogs missing, they would undoubtedly have discovered it yesterday and got in touch. 'I'll ring you later,' he promised before he hung up.

Now that the initial shock of receiving so unwelcome a gift was over, his veterinarian brain began functioning. It was a dog and it was dead. Dogs rarely died for no discoverable cause. He moved the shoe-box with its sad contents to one side and covered the worktop with a sheet of thickish plastic—the sort of thing that had been kept for no better reason than that it might come in useful some day. For once, 'some day' had come. The teeth suggested that it was quite a young dog and, he noted, heavily undershot, which suggested it was no show animal: exhibitors and to a lesser extent breeders tended to avoid animals whose front teeth did not meet in the so-called scissor-bite, with the top incisors overlapping snugly against the lower ones. In some breeds, such as Bulldogs, the pugnacious thrusting forward of the lower jaw so that it not only overlapped the upper but left a slight gap as well was a requirement. In breeds which Linus would describe as having 'normal' heads, such undershooting was regarded as a serious fault. The dog before him had a profile like a pugilist. Linus's post-mortem revealed nothing to account for a death from natural causes. There was naturally a limit to how much he could ascertain under these conditions, but it showed no signs of trauma such as would be associated with a road accident; nothing was broken and there was no sign of any abnormality of the internal organs that might account for an early death.

When he had found out all he could, he wrapped it neatly up and replaced it in its cardboard coffin, tying the lid on before placing the whole thing in the fridge. Then he telephoned the home number of a forensic friend engaged in research at the Cambridge veterinary school. Next day he despatched the little dog by Red Star and awaited results.

His actions had all been very practical, no doubt, but the one thing they couldn't do was explain who had sent him the dog or why. Linus was perfectly capable of hazarding an educated guess at both. The very choice of breed pointed the finger in the direction which could not possibly have been taken had it been a Poodle or a Peke. He suspected that, since the claque had not succeeded in putting him off showing, this might be the next attempt. The claque had been unpleasant and unsporting but it had at least been—he searched for the right word—*human*. This was not. It was inhuman and quite possibly insane. It was so extreme and unbalanced a course of action that he wondered whether it had ever been employed before and, if so, why nothing had been done about it. If it had not been tried before, he wondered why it should have been the weapon used in his case.

If its purpose was to persuade him to abandon any interest in AVDs in general or Helen's dogs in particular, it wasn't very difficult to guess from which direction it had come. It was purely circumstantial to associate it with the claque but there was no other body of people in the breed whom he considered capable of doing such a thing. To pin it down more precisely was more difficult. He had a shrewd idea it could never be traced to Morwenna Leyburn. She was far too clever to allow herself to be caught like that. Her technique was more likely to have been that of Henry II: a general entreaty to be rid of this turbulent priest that would enable her to disclaim responsibility on the grounds that it wasn't intended to be taken seriously. Nick Fidden was a likely candidate for a favour-currying knight but he certainly wasn't the only one.

Such thoughts were inevitable and there was no denying that Morwenna Leyburn and her followers were nothing if not weird, and were generally held to be so both within and without the breed of their choice. All the same, it was one thing to be weird and quite another to be deranged. Linus, like Ishmael, was hard to prise loose from something once his teeth were sunk into it. He was not going to give up showing Helen's dogs—at least, not until it suited him to do so—but he could not deny a feeling of unease so strong that, despite instructions to the contrary, he started taking Ishmael to work with him. It was not that he feared for his own safety and felt the dog would be a protection. It was for Ishmael's safety he feared. If someone was prepared to kill an unidentified dog to send to him, as he suspected they must have done, then the next discouragement was likely to be the death of his own pet. The Ministry might not like it but the Ministry would have to put up with it. He hoped it would prove to be temporary.

At that weekend's show the judge was a breed specialist: the girl Linus had first seen wearing a man's evening suit. She wore black to judge. Dead black relieved only by heavy gold earrings. It was the first time Linus had ever seen a black sari. He was not altogether surprised to find Munchkin was thrown out with the rubbish—a devastating expression which simply meant he did not win any prize, however humble. He was rather more taken aback to find that no one was inclined to talk to him save Mrs Curbridge, and she seemed more reluctant than on previous occasions. Linus tried to remember whether he had said anything to offend her but he could think of nothing so he assumed she had no wish to rock a boat over which the Morwenna Leyburn crowd had so much control. Since he had no intention of remaining in the breed indefinitely, he decided it would be unfair to push an acquaintance which, however superficial, she now seemed to have no desire to pursue so he made no effort to involve her in unwelcome conversation.

He had a phone call from his forensic friend that evening.

'Sorry I've taken so long,' he said. 'As a matter of fact, I gave it to some of my students. Thought it would do them good to carry out an autopsy on a dog about whose veterinary history they knew nothing. Very interesting it proved. I don't suppose you'd like to tell me what you know about it?'

'Absolutely nothing,' Linus told him. 'You already know all that I know. My own PM showed nothing—I told you that—and I just don't know anything about the dog's history.'

'Then what made you so interested?'

'The one thing I didn't tell you: I received it in the post. An unsolicited gift, you might say.'

The forensic man whistled. 'Nasty,' he commented. 'In the circumstances, very nasty. If I were you, old boy, I'd be very, very careful. Someone out there doesn't much like you.'

Linus suddenly felt a little shaky but he kept his voice steady. 'That won't be for the first time,' he said. 'What did the dog die of?'

'You won't altogether believe this. I didn't myself at first. The poor little blighter was killed with curare—injected into its jugular vein. What do you make of that?'

'Nothing very nice.'

'Quite. Let me know what it's all about some time, will you? In the meantime, sweet dreams.'

Linus replaced the handset thoughtfully. There were many drugs appropriate for putting down small animals. Curare was not one of them. Furthermore, any of the others would be more easily obtainable than that exotic substance simply because every vet carried them. There might even be the careless, unprofessional vet who handed a phial over to an owner so that the owner could do the job himself. He hoped not, but it wasn't unknown. More probably the source would be an unlocked car or an unobserved bag. No vet carried curare. Linus wasn't even sure if he could have got hold of some even if he had needed it. Nor did one destroy dogs by injecting into the jugular vein. The usual way was into a vein in the front leg. Very occasionally and in certain circumstances, an injection straight into the heart.

No, there was a symbolic element to the killing of that little dog. Every reader of travellers' tales knew that curare was a South American drug, that Amazonian Indians tipped their darts with it. What could be more fitting than that it should be used on an Amazonian Vampire Dog—even if the breed's connection with the Amazon basin was more than a little spurious? The use of the jugular vein tied in nicely with Vampire legend relating to the breed and one of its more irritating—or endearing, depending on your point of view—habits. Linus dismissed the possibility that there was a further connection in the fact that much of his professional time these days was spent in putting down cows by precisely that method. That was an ironic coincidence. It was unlikely that anyone connected with AVDs would be aware of it.

He was disinclined to take too much notice of his friend's warning. He already knew he was none too popular in certain circles. He could not quite see how anyone was going to get close enough to him for long enough to inject curare into his jugular vein. He did find himself wondering how they got hold of the stuff, though. Hospitals would have it, of course. It was sometimes used in anaesthesia. Hospitals also kept such drugs under very careful security both in terms of locks and checks. Still, it was reasonable to assume that must be the source. He would have to keep his ears open for any hint of a connection, however tenuous, between the AVD exhibitors and the medical profession.

He tried to put the details of this recent unpleasant development out of his mind and succeeded on a superficial level, though his spirits, depressed by receiving such an unwanted gift in the first place, sank lower with this new information.

Two days later the postman delivered to Government Buildings a padded envelope addressed to Mr L. Rintoul, MRCVS, for personal attention. It was therefore not opened by anyone else. There was a box inside, small but very rigid. Linus's stomach shifted a little when he saw it but it really was too small to contain a Vampire Dog. He put his finger under the sticky tape. Except a puppy, he thought suddenly and lifted the lid reluctantly. He need not have worried. There was no Amazonian Vampire Dog inside.

Instead there was a small figure, apparently made of candle-wax. It was unmistakably male. And it had three pins sticking out of its tiny neck.

Linus jammed the lid down very quickly, as if by hiding if from view he might forget its existence. It crossed his mind as he listened to the sound of his own heart thumping that the sender might have been better advised to stick the pins in that part of the figure's anatomy. It did not cross his mind that the model represented anyone except himself. He picked up the envelope. This time the postmark was perfectly clear but singularly unhelpful. It had been posted on the previous day. In London. Nice, safe, vast, anonymous London.

He had a vague recollection that one or two of the AVD people lived in the capital and he could easily check it against the catalogues of the shows he had attended, but that would mean very little. Anyone within commuter range of the city could have popped up with it if they'd needed to. Even more easily, provided it had been stamped, they could have handed it to a neighbour and asked him to slip it into the first pillar-box he encountered.

If anyone had mentioned to Linus a few days ago the possibly baneful effects of little wax dolls with pins in, he would have laughed it off as superstitious nonsense. He still believed it was superstitious nonsense to imagine that such a thing could have a real physical effect upon the recipient—he was a vet, after all, a trained scientific mind. But he no longer laughed it off. The receipt of that figure had unnerved him in a way the dead dog had not. The dog came within his own experience. It had been unpleasant to receive it and even more unpleasant to learn of the manner of its death, but apart from the probable symbolism involved and that was straightforward enough—it was scientifically explicable, its only purpose to shock. This was different. It wasn't so much a matter of whether *he* thought it would work, but the fact that the sender presumably thought so.

His hand hovered over the telephone. Wasn't this the sort of thing they brought the police in for? He withdrew his hand. Quite possibly it was, but he had a constitutional dislike of appearing a fool. He didn't think he was one, but nor was he entirely sure. Linus Rintoul might very well strike others as self-contained and confident and in some respects that was true enough. In others he was surprisingly diffident—in his relationships with women, for instance. Certainly his self-assurance was not so well developed that he could view with equanimity the prospect of a policeman, particularly not some fresh-faced young constable, inquiring into his reasons for fearing that a bunch of elderly hippies were trying to get him out of a breed of dog he wasn't even seriously into. It was a fair bet the policeman wouldn't even consider the dog-game to be something to be taken all that seriously in the first place.

He didn't phone.

Later that evening he rang Sean and asked his son if he knew any theological students.

'I'm reading engineering, Dad,' Sean said patiently. 'There's not a lot of connection.'

'I realize that. I just thought you might happen to know some. One, anyway.'

'Not that I can think of. Why? I didn't know you were interested in the church.'

'I'm not. It's just that there was something I wanted to know about and, not being a churchgoer, I didn't want to bother the local vicar.'

'What was it?' Sean was clearly intrigued.

'It's not all that important. I'll see you around. Look after yourself.'

The abrupt ending would surprise Sean and it would probably upset him but Linus was in no mood to explain either what had happened or the fears and apprehensions it had aroused. He thought of the young, stolid policeman accompanying Netley, and his entirely unexpected comment about the rooks. It was a pity he didn't know his name. Linus had the feeling that the young man might take this sort of thing seriously. However, he could think of no way of contacting him without going through the normal channels and that was something he had already decided against. He slept uneasily that night.

He found next day that his attitude to the post had changed. He viewed both the incoming mail at work and the letters waiting for him on the mat at home with a quickened heart-beat and a fair degree of apprehension. This was unpleasantly disconcerting. He had always seen himself as a down-to-earth, no-nonsense sort of chap and although he knew in his heart there were areas where that image was a bit blurred around the edges, it was unnerving to find it quite so effectively shattered.

He thought of Helen. Dead in bizarre circumstances that at first suggested heart-failure but which were now known to be a heroin overdose. Linus could not believe she had been in the habit of dosing herself with heroin. Impasse.

There was an undoubted connection between Helen and Mr Justice Wingfield. No—two; the terrorist trial and the world of AVDs. It was inconceivable that the competitive jealousies of the dog-game should result in murder but it was also inconceivable that disgruntled terrorists should arrange for their victims to be found in such bizarre circumstances. The judge, for example, might well have died of entirely natural causes, however induced, yet he could not possibly have put himself into the position in which he was found. In the same way, it mattered little whether Helen had also died of a heart attack or had OD'd—in neither situation would she have been likely to go to Silbury Hill and take her clothes off. It was these extraordinary elements which reinforced Linus's opinion that AVD people must have been behind both deaths, even though murder was a remarkably drastic step to take simply to prevent certain people judging. Perhaps the original idea had been to frighten the judges into relinquishing the appointment and, in Mr Justice Wingfield's case, the frightening had gone too far? A little further thought told him that, if the method had been to send dead dogs to the Judge, he would have been more likely simply to call in the police but that, if the shock had killed him, he would have been found dead at home. Still, in that eventuality, the police would have found the canine corpse and doubtless pursued the connection.

No matter how Linus looked at the puzzle, he went inconclusively round and round it, like a man trying unsuccessfully to get out of a maze, knowing the solution must be simple and possibly even self-evident, but unable to find it. He had little doubt that the contents of his own post-bag were designed to make him drop his own recent interest in the breed and had no hesitation in attributing them to Morwenna Leyburn and her cohorts. He had no problems with his own heart, despite being of an age when they might be expected, but the palpitations with which he approached his entirely unexceptional mail made him realize that it might not take very much more of this sort of thing before one sudden shock would be enough to finish him off, too.

Helen had made no mention of any unpleasantnesses arriving through the post, admitting only to one threatening phone call at the time of the trial. She seemed to have been able to dismiss that call without too much difficulty, probably because she knew she had not been the only recipient. Linus thought of his own reluctance to discuss what had happened with anyone else. Why shouldn't Helen have felt equally reluctant if she too had had similarly distasteful gifts? He didn't think he was being unduly conceited to believe that, if she had told anyone, it would have been he, not because of their closeness—which he had perhaps rated higher than she—but because she had talked to him so much about her feelings concerning Vampire Dogs and the other people involved with them. He knew of no one else in whom she might have confided. She seemed not to have had any very close friends at all and had almost certainly been entirely unaware of the existence of Mrs Muckross, the only relative the police had managed to trace.

Mrs Muckross. There was something about the recollection of that personification of thin, grey respectability that niggled at the corners of his mind like a quotation whose attribution eluded him. He worried it about for a bit without success and then left it. If he immersed himself in work, maybe whatever it was would surface unexpectedly in the course of the day.

* * *

In view of his phone call to Sean, it was ironic that the next day's work should include a visit to a vicarage at the other end of the district. The vicar and his wife had decided that a few 'ornamental' sheep would be useful in keeping down the grass in the vast old garden and perhaps—if the parishioners weren't offended—in the graveyard as well. It would have been an eminently practical idea had the couple not been young, enthusiastic and so new to country life that they simply hadn't realized that there was rather more to keeping sheep—even ornamental ones—than a patch of grass and a bucket of water. A farmer who was also a parish councillor had suggested to Trevarrick, Linus's boss, that a visit from the Ministry wearing its educational hat might be better for the sheep than interference from a farmer who had already had cause to draw the vicar's attention to one or two practical shortcomings in his handling of parish politics. The Divisional Veterinary Officer decided that that particular hat best fitted Linus.

The couple were eager enough to learn and dismayed at the extent of their ignorance, and when Linus suggested that they could do no better than to consult the farmer who had asked him to visit—though Linus diplomatically didn't mention this last fact—they screwed up their noses and exchanged glances.

'One of my severest critics, I'm afraid,' the vicar said.

'Is he?' Linus gave a good imitation of surprise. 'He knows sheep, though, and people love to be asked about the things at which they excel. You might even find that asking him about your sheep would lay the foundations of a better relationship.'

The vicar conceded that that might well be the case and invited Linus in for coffee. The conversation began with sheep and then became more general, and Linus became very much aware that the vicar's wife wore a rather unusual cross, a far cry from the customary discreet little bit of gold one usually saw. It was large and grey and covered in geometrically interlocking circles superimposed on a trellis. He eyed it from time to time before deciding to overrule his mother's instruction that one never commented upon someone's appearance or possessions unless invited to do so.

'An unusual cross,' he remarked. 'I don't think I've ever seen one quite like it. Most attractive.'

The young woman was surprised but not displeased. 'Do you like it? I'm so glad. Most people don't. It's pewter—American pewter. An aunt brought it back for me years ago and I've always loved it.'

'I'm not surprised,' Linus said truthfully. 'I met a woman a few weeks ago with an equally unusual design, though not modern like that. It was a cross with a loop at the top. An ankh, I think she said it was. I may not have that quite right but it was something like that.'

The vicar frowned. 'No, you've remembered it correctly. Nothing to do with Christianity, I'm afraid. It's Egyptian originally—the emblem of Ka, the spiritual double of man. It's supposed to be the symbol of life.'

'That's why it was familiar,' Linus said with the air of one for whom a mystery has been unravelled. 'I spend quite a bit of time in the Ashmolean. I've probably seen it there. Why do you frown? Do you disapprove of people wearing the symbol of life? It seems quite a nice idea to me.'

'Put like that, I suppose it is, apart from its essential paganism, of which I'm sure you wouldn't expect me to approve. No, it's not that. It's become associated with witchcraft and I think you can assume that anyone wearing it these days is very likely to be involved.'

'I can see that the Church wouldn't like that,' Linus admitted. 'Still, it is the old religion of these shores, isn't it? And can't it be used for good as well as the evil we associate with it?'

'So they will tell you and I don't doubt there's an element of that in it, at least for some people. There's no denying the fact that it tends to attract the unstable personalities—those with a basic tendency towards a combination of weakness and viciousness, the sort of person who dreams of having power—or at least the illusion of power—and there's no denying witchcraft gives that. All that communing with the elements.'

'To say nothing of little wax models with pins in,' Linus contributed and was surprised that he found it quite difficult to utter the words, even in so general a context. 'Do those things actually work?'

The vicar looked at him a little more intently. 'I'm not sure. This isn't my field. You'd really need to ask a specialist. The rector of Long Blessington is the one to tell you. There's supposed to be a long history of witchcraft associated with that village. So far as wax models are concerned, I suppose a lot depends upon the temperament of the recipient. I suspect that, if someone gets one and believes it will work, then it probably will. It's psychological, you see.'

'That makes sense,' Linus agreed. 'It might work on someone who wasn't too bright, or who was guided more by their emotions than by their logic. I can't imagine it having much effect on, say, a nuclear physicist.'

The vicar shook his head. 'Don't kid yourself. It's a matter of the type of personality rather than its intelligence or education. If you're worried about it, why don't you go over to Long Blessington? I'll give the rector there a ring if you like.'

'Oh, I'm not worried,' Linus said hastily. Too hastily, perhaps. 'Just curious.'

'Well, I think you're making too much of it,' the vicar's wife declared. 'After all, anyone who's ever sat up to watch a late-night horror movie knows all about little wax models and I bet there are idiots who send them just for fun in the hope of frightening someone—possibly even someone they actually like—but with no real wish to do harm. That's not witchcraft.'

'That's just pure stupidity,' her husband said. 'I'm sure you're right and that happens, but it's like playing with a ouija board—you can never be quite sure of the consequences. You couldn't be sure whether the person you sent it to would receive it in the spirit in which it was sent. It's called playing with fire.'

'You seem to take it quite seriously,' Linus commented, troubled. He had expected the vicar to laugh it all off as superstition.

'Anything in which a large body of people believes should be taken seriously,' the vicar replied. 'And, in any case, why not? My religion depends very heavily upon a belief in a force for good, a force which we believe can be influenced by prayer. Surely it is only logical to assume that there must also be a force for evil? If one accepts that premise, is there any reason to doubt that it, too, can be influenced by intercession, entreaty, prayer—call it what you will—from those who wish to enlist its aid?'

Linus was an atheist and quite often an agnostic as well, though he was never quite so sure upon that point. Had the vicar referred to a belief in God, he would have been able to reject the rest of that gentleman's argument. The vicar had been cleverer than that, perhaps by instinct, perhaps by shrewd psychology, and Linus was bound to admit that his arguments had a certain logic about them that was difficult to refute. The conversation had got a little deeper than he had intended and he had an uncomfortable feeling that the vicar suspected his interest was more than academic. He looked at his watch.

'I'm not sure that I agree with your premise, though I see your line of reasoning. I'd like to continue the discussion some day, but in the meantime I've a farm to visit at Henley. Thanks for the coffee. It was very welcome.'

'As are you, Mr Rintoul. Any time you want to talk—but don't forget the rector of Long Blessington. He's likely to be more help than me.'

Linus knew then that the young cleric might not know much about sheep, but he was not easily fooled where people were concerned.

* * *

The mind works in peculiar ways and Linus had a sneaking suspicion his only functioned at night. He had pushed Mrs Muckross's name to the back of his mind so thoroughly that he would have sworn he had forgotten all about whatever it had been that he hadn't quite been able to put his finger on. At some godforsaken hour he was suddenly awake and perfectly well aware what his finger had been searching for.

Among Helen's canine records had been that diary. He had glanced at it and it had appeared to contain nothing more than fuller accounts of things to do with the dogs, particularly veterinary matters and dietary changes—the sort of diary that anyone with a scientific training might be expected to keep in order to monitor progress. He had no idea whether Helen had also kept the more conventional kind of diary. If she had, and if she had mentioned any sinister occurrences in it, the police would presumably have kept it and be pursuing some inquiries in that direction, though comments that had been made suggested that their thoughts were still on a connection between Mr Justice Wingfield and Helen through the trial. Was it conceivable that they hadn't read the canine diary from cover to cover? That they, like Linus, had flipped over the pages, read a few of them and decided it wasn't relevant? It was possible but surely improbable. Yet, if Helen didn't keep a more conventional journal, where else might she record events, particularly since they were connected with the dogs? He wanted that diary. In the morning he would ring Mrs Muckross.

Helen's only traceable relative did not greet his voice with exclamations of delight.

'Have you found homes for those dogs yet, Mr Rintoul?' she asked. 'I've had one or two interested people ringing me up and, frankly, I'm beginning to regret that I let you have them. I've been offered very good prices for them, particularly if I throw in their papers—which, of course, I'm unable to do because I handed them over to you.'

'If the inquirers are the people I think they are, I can assure you Helen would not have wanted them to have her dogs,' Linus told her with perfect truth.

Mrs Muckross sighed. 'Since I didn't know

Helen and don't know the dogs, that consideration is of limited importance so far as I'm concerned. Right now I'd like to be rid of the whole business.'

'Which is precisely why I'm phoning you,' Linus said. 'Among Helen's kennel papers was a diary relating to the dogs. I didn't take it because it didn't seem to me at the time to be relevant to anyone except Helen, but I wonder if I could come over and collect it? I think I may need it after all.'

'Why?' It was, in the circumstances, an entirely reasonable question.

'We're having a bit of a problem with their food,' Linus lied. 'Well, quite a major problem, actually. They seem to be allergic to something. Now I flicked over the pages of that diary and there were one or two comments about changes in diet that she'd introduced—you'll find them for yourself if you care to look—and I'm hoping the diary will give me some clue as to how to deal with it.'

'I thought you said you were a vet?' she said suspiciously.

'I am. With the Ministry of Agriculture. You're welcome to check if you doubt it.'

'If you're a vet and it's a matter of diet, I should have thought you'd have been perfectly capable of getting to the bottom of it yourself.'

'Indeed I am,' Linus assured her. 'The trouble is, they're such very little dogs that it won't take much in the way of a tummy upset or loss of appetite to finish one of them off and I'm hoping the clues are there in Helen's book to enable me to act before we get to that stage.'

Linus knew the story was plausible. It remained to be seen whether it was convincing. There was a long pause.

'Hmm. Well, in that case . . . Will it suit you if I put it in the post this afternoon?'

'Would you mind if I came to collect it after work? I do feel time is of the essence and the posts are so unreliable these days. Quite apart from any probable delay, it would be so awful if it went entirely astray, don't you think? I promise you I'll return it as soon as I've had a chance to read the relevant bits and make a note of them.'

Mrs Muckross was plainly unhappy with the suggestion, but she agreed.

* * *

Linus made himself comfortable on the sofa with a mug of cocoa in one hand and Helen's diary in the other. It was late, but he knew there was no point in going to bed until he had read it. It covered a period of several years, most of which were of no interest to him since he was looking chiefly for events since her arrival in Long Blessington. He recalled her having said that things had not been exactly friendly before that, but he rather thought that any more serious unpleasantness was likely to have started after she came to this area: had it occurred before, he thought she might have tackled it one way or another and either defeated it or been defeated by it.

He scanned the pages until he came to her record of having been to see the cottage and finding it exactly what she wanted. It contained references to exactly where she could place kennelling and exercise runs. This struck him as odd, since during his acquaintance with her the dogs had always been in the house, though there was kennelling outside, much as she had described.

The diary was strictly factual but as the account progressed, the choice of words in which it was couched hinted at an increasingly unhappy spirit. Following her first win after moving to the cottage, she received a phone call telling her that was her last stroke of good luck in the breed, and here she commented that previous 'heavy breathing' phone calls which had frequently followed the success of one of her dogs might have been from the same source although, at the time, she had never connected them with a show—they had always come towards the end of a weekend and she had assumed it was some nutter at a loose end on a Sunday night. She had not recognized the voice. A further phone call warning her not to go to a certain show led to her bringing the dogs into the house, thus explaining the empty kennels. She recorded her revulsion at receiving, as Linus had, a dead Vampire Dog. Hers had been a slightly premature and therefore presumably a stillborn puppy, but unlike Linus's it had the added refinement of a small tag tied round its neck upon which was printed her affix—the registered name that identifies one breeder's dogs from another. Now she began to use the diary as much to record her thoughts as to set down the facts of her kennel management. Linus decided that the very fact that she, with her scientific training, did this was an indication of the extent to which events were affecting her.

Helen's next unwanted gift was, like Linus's, a wax model with pins in it, but unlike his, these were in the heart. At this stage she considered calling the police, something Linus would have advised her to do after getting the puppy, though he had not subsequently taken his own advice when he found himself in a similar situation. Her reasons for not doing so were similar to his own. Fear of ridicule had stopped her, just as it had stopped him. She was also still hopeful that she would eventually be accepted by the Leyburn faction and guessed—undoubtedly correctly—that she could whistle that down the wind once the police started asking questions. It was Linus's opinion that appeasement was far less effective than outright confrontation, since the aggressor always came out on top.

Then the diary told him something that did surprise him. She had consulted the Long Blessington rector. Linus was surprised because this had happened after he had met her, yet he had never had the slightest suspicion that anything was worrying her to quite that extent, even though it was the unexplained illness of her dogs—the illness that had caused her to approach him in the pub—that had finally sent her to the rector.

The clergyman hadn't belittled her fears but he had pointed out to her that anyone who watched a late-night movie knew all about little wax models; it was the one aspect of Black Magic, along with saying the Lord's Prayer backwards, that everyone had heard of, and that there was actually considerably more to the Old Religion than that. It was therefore quite possible that the person behind these unpleasant events, knowing the reputation of the Long Blessington contingent, was deliberately using the methods that people would associate with Morwenna and her crowd. This, Helen admitted both to the rector and her diary, had not occurred to her. It was a reasonable suggestion but she knew the personalities involved and really couldn't believe any of them were capable of such a thing. She had no such reservations about Morwenna. She considered—and dismissed—the possibility that this was the devious way the terrorists' friends had chosen to wreak their revenge. Terrorists hit their targets in far less oblique ways.

Linus stopped reading at this point to do his own mental review of the other Vampire Dog people and even allowing for the fact that the most improbable people do the most unlikely things, he was forced to agree with Helen.

The rector recommended the use of prayer 'at this stage'. Helen felt it could do little harm and might conceivably do some good, but she clearly had little real faith in its efficacy and was, Linus suspected, disappointed that the rector had not been able to make a more concrete suggestion. Had he told her to go to the police, Linus rather thought she would have done.

The female wax model was followed after an interval by a similar one of a dog which seemed to have unnerved Helen much more. She dreaded the postman's visit, recording much the same physical phenomena that Linus had already observed in himself. However, Helen had gone on to become much more fearful. Around the time that she decided not to see him for a while, she was—contradictorily—afraid to be alone in the house at night and Linus learned that one of the reasons for her having decided they should see less of each other was that she was determined to conquer what she saw as an irrational fear and felt she was becoming too dependent upon his company and his support.

Linus closed the diary thoughtfully. He had found out what he wanted to know. Helen had been subjected to a similar campaign to the one he was suffering but hers had gone much further. She had been in no doubt at all that its purpose was to get her out of the breed in which she posed such a threat to the opposition, and she was pig-headedly determined not to go. Linus could only feel deeply sorry that she had not felt able to confide in him. He had no idea in what way he could have helped her, but she would surely have found it easier to cope with once she had a sympathetic ally. The diary naturally made no mention of her reason for having gone without him on that fateful morning. He had no idea whether she had gone to Silbury Hill on her own initiative or had gone somewhere else—perhaps to meet someone—and been taken there. He would not have been surprised if she had had a heart attack. After so much careful conditioning it might have taken only one cleverly stage-managed shock to induce one, especially if she was not psychologically prepared for exactly that. And oddly enough, despite the pins, it seemed she wasn't. Throughout her account she seemed to have believed that the sole purpose was to persuade her to give up her chosen breed. Linus had no doubt at all that, had she done so, the incidents would have stopped, but she seemed to have given no thought to the question of how far her persecutors might be prepared to go, apparently believing that she only had to stick it out and they would either accept her or—more probably—simply give up.

Linus would be well advised to learn from that particular mistake.

He put the diary tidily down on the coffee-table, absent-mindedly aligning it with the corner. Then he took his mug into the kitchen, rinsed it out and refilled it with water to stand until morning. This, too, he placed neatly at the far corner of the draining-board. He hated kitchen clutter at the best of times; first thing in the morning was never the best of times. It hadn't bothered his wife, a fact which had been a bone of contention between them, a focus of anger when the real cause of irritation had been less easy to mention.

He lay in bed staring up at the ceiling. He wouldn't have been able to sleep if he hadn't read the diary first. Now that he had done so, he still couldn't because of all the questions it raised. Chief among these was the very crucial one of whether the police had read—really read—the diary. Linus didn't have a great regard for the police though there were individual policemen—of whom Inspector

Lacock was one—for whom he had considerable respect. Even so, it was hard to believe that they had missed so vital a piece of evidence. They hadn't missed it entirely, of course: they had handed it along with all the other kennel documentation to Mrs Muckross. Helen had been both orderly and organized. All the papers relating to the dogs would have been kept in one place and been carefully labelled. Perhaps that had put the police off the scent. Perhaps they, like Linus, had simply flicked through the pages initially, dipping in here and there, finding nothing more relevant to their inquiries than the fact that on a certain day Mopsy had half a mil of Penbritin or Munchkin had declined his minced tripe. Linus's own cursory examination had not turned up any reference beyond that sort of thing. It was not until he began to read the later parts of the journal properly that he discovered something more sinister was happening.

At the time the police went through Helen's papers, they were looking for—or at least, on the lookout for—anything that might tie her death into that of Mr Justice Wingfield and the trial in which they had each played their part. There was naturally nothing to connect them in Helen's kennel records and what appeared to be nothing more than a dry account of food and drugs, temperatures and whelping intervals, might well not have seemed worth closer scrutiny. If that were the explanation, it probably said more about police manning levels than their inefficiency and Linus wondered whether he ought not to hand the book over to them first thing in the morning.

There wasn't really much to wonder about. He had no real doubts about where his duty lay but even as he acknowledged that, he knew he wouldn't do it, at least not yet. He would put the diary in a safe place, somewhere where it would be found if anything happened to him and he would take the precaution of making sure it had a note attached to it to draw someone's attention to the relevant parts. Then he would dig a lot deeper and a lot more deliberately into the whole world of these Vampire Dogs until he had the whole thing gift-wrapped and labelled and fit to be handed over to the proper authorities who had so far been so careless. Besides, he didn't like having his hand forced and that is what someone was trying to do.

CHAPTER EIGHT

There was only one more show for which Helen had entered her dogs and they could not then be entered for any more until they had been transferred to new ownership. Linus had little doubt that Mrs Muckross could be persuaded to transfer them to his name or the Thelwalls, but neither he nor they really wanted them. So far Morwenna had been the only person to exhibit any interest in acquiring them but that might have been because others felt more diffident about appearing to be scavenging among the bones. He really ought to start sounding them out but he had no desire for Morwenna or her cronies to get wind of it. Somehow or other he must contrive a bombshell and drop it, confident that that way he might betray someone into revealing the truth about what happened to Helen. The nature of the bombshell remained to be seen.

Whether it was fear, suppressed excitement or simply the knowledge that he had made up his mind about a course of action and was following it, Linus wasn't sure, but his spirits and with them, his mood, were very much on the *qui vive* that day. That fact did not go unnoticed.

'You seem very cheerful this morning,' Mrs Curbridge remarked.

Morwenna Leyburn was closer to the mark. 'My, we are spunky today,' she said with her inimitable ability to make a snide comment without appearing to do so.

Linus just smiled sweetly and had the satisfaction of seeing her turn away with just the hint of a frown.

'You do seem to have a knack of irritating Morwenna,' Mrs Curbridge commented, taking care to pitch her voice too low for it to carry. 'I sometimes wonder if it's deliberate.'

'I don't think so,' Linus said, surprised. 'It's entirely unplanned, I assure you—she doesn't much like me and detests the fact that I'm here to stay.'

Mrs Curbridge shook her head. 'I don't think that's the whole story,' she said. 'Perhaps you don't even realize you're doing it. My first husband had exactly the same ability and our son inherited it, only happily Matt never directs it at me.' She laughed with the embarrassed self-consciousness of one who only rarely speaks of matters close to them.

'Perhaps you're right,' Linus agreed, anxious to guide her over that embarrassment. She was, after all, the only really pleasant person—other than Helen—associated with the breed.

'So you're sticking with the breed?' she went on, happy to change the subject back again.

'I think so,' he said, his tone denying any doubt implicit in the words. 'I've a hunch that the key to Helen's death lies here somewhere, though I don't think the police share that view.'

'Oh dear, I do hope you're mistaken. Have you spoken to them about it?'

'I suppose it did sound like that. I merely meant that they don't seem to be pursuing inquiries in this quarter, do they?'

'I'm sure they know what they're doing,' Mrs Curbridge protested gently. 'They're the professionals, after all.'

'I try to remember that, but I sometimes wonder whether someone less ... official ... might not be more successful.'

Mrs Curbridge looked around her as if what she was about to impart were of considerable significance. 'Let sleeping dogs lie is my maxim,' she confided.

Linus sighed. 'Wouldn't that be nice? I think it's a matter of personality—I always have to root around until I get to the bottom of things even though I know it would usually be more sensible to let well alone.'

The judge was another all-rounder, one who prided himself on his expert knowledge of the rarer breeds, with most of which he had, at best, a passing acquaintance—which, as one cynic observed to Linus, meant that he could usually tell which breed was which on a good day.

How true that unkind comment might be Linus was not sufficiently well-informed himself to judge, but there was little doubt the man knew which were the important faces in the breed and, just in case he was in any doubt, the claque was out in force, cheering their candidates along and preserving a significant silence while other dogs were being examined. Linus found it easier to bear this time, partly bcause it was not such a shock and partly because it was not directed solely at the dogs he was handling.

To any student of human nature, the judging would have been extremely interesting. From time to time the judge asserted his independence. In Novice Dog and Novice Bitch and again in Special Beginner's Dog, he placed against the claque, but Linus had been exhibiting long enough by now to know that these classes, wins in which did not carry a Crufts qualifier, were not regarded as of great significance by seasoned exhibitors. He noticed that the claque was sufficiently magnanimously disposed towards the winners of these classes to clap them politely, thus preserving a façade of good sportsmanship. Munchkin took a non-qualifying Reserve in Limit Dog and was unplaced in Open. Yum-Yum managed nothing more than Very Highly Commended. Linus made a point of congratulating the winners with an affability that earned him a highly suspicious glance from both Morwenna and Fidden.

Back at the benches, Morwenna exuded charm and sympathy.

'That was really very bad luck,' she commiserated. 'I do think you should have been better placed than that. The dogs were looking quite nice, too.'

Linus could be charming when it suited him. His smile was undimmed. 'I thought we were a little unlucky,' he agreed, 'but then, that's the name of the game, isn't it? And it's not as if they weren't both qualified already. I think I can afford not to begrudge it to someone else.'

'How very generous—I wish more people saw it like that!' She paused. 'After all the work you've put into poor Helen's dogs, it seems a pity they won't actually be able to go to Crufts—not without being transferred to someone else's name.'

'It would be a pity, wouldn't it?' Linus agreed. 'Fortunately that won't happen.' He had the satisfaction of seeing the smile disappear.

'Why? What do you mean?'

'Hadn't you realized? I'm taking them over. Not entirely on my own, of course. The Thelwalls—you remember David Thelwall, I expect? The vet at Enstone?' Morwenna indicated that she did. 'He and his wife are coming into partnership with me. They're very taken with them, but of course they don't have time to show them, so I'll go on doing that. I live alone, you know. It will give me an interest and, anyway, I think Helen would have wanted it.' God! he thought. How pi can one man sound? Morwenna's face told him he had dropped the bombshell he had sought.

She clutched at the sides of the crater that had opened beneath her feet. 'But you won't be able to. I mean, they have to be transferred into your names and that requires Helen's signature.'

'Or her heir's. I checked with the Kennel Club. The police traced a relative—some kind of second cousin, I believe, and she was quite happy to sign them over to us.' Linus had a notion it might be safer for Mrs Muckross if the transfer was believed to be a *fait accompli*.

'You've seen this relative?'

'Why, yes. Didn't she tell you? She told me about you.'

Morwenna rallied herself with a deliberate expansion of her smile. 'So we shall be seeing a lot more of you. Nick,' she called out, beckoning him across. 'You'll never guess what Mr Rintoul has just told me. It seems he's taking over Helen's dogs. They've been transferred to his name. Apparently that relative was quite happy to let him have them. Isn't that lucky?'

Fidden scowled, an expression that did nothing to enhance his cadaverous features. 'You must be a glutton for punishment,' he said.

Linus looked at him innocently. 'Why? What do you mean?' He didn't think it was entirely his imagination that a warning glance passed between them.

Fidden shrugged. 'Only that you have to be more than a bit mad to want to get involved with this game.'

'D'you know, that was exactly the conclusion I'd come to,' Linus told him blandly, and saw Mrs Curbridge shaking her head at him in saddened admonishment.

* * *

The parking space at Enstone was outside the quarantine kennels and not visible from the bungalow itself, which meant that Linus had to carry the dogs and their show paraphernalia some distance to the back door. Ruth let him in.

'You'll stay for supper,' she said. The invitation was always extended and Linus always accepted it. He felt a bit guilty about it because it was beginning to look as if he were taking it for granted, and that could provoke a resentment that might ultimately spell the end of a friendship. He really must do something to repay their hospitality. The obvious thing would be to take them out for a slap-up meal but the nature of their business meant that someone had to be on the premises twenty-four hours a day—and not just anyone: an employee would do, a neighbour (if there were one) wouldn't. It made evenings out so difficult to arrange that Ruth and David tended not to bother except for special celebrations, such as their wedding anniversary. A case of wine might perhaps be appropriate. It would be a small enough price to pay for what was invariably a very good meal in very congenial company. When the Vampire Dogs were gone, he would miss these suppers.

Ruth Thelwall was not a farmer's daughter for nothing. She was very well aware of the importance of what Linus always thought of as good, honest English food. In this instance, a steak-and-kidney pudding in to which, he was delighted to note, she had not committed the cardinal sin of putting onions. Accompanied by sprouts and mashed potato, it was almost certainly bad for him, but then, everything was these days, so Linus tucked in with his customary gusto.

'How did it go?' David asked once the initial pangs had been placated.

Linus told him. 'I've a confession to make,' he added, guiltily realizing that he had committed the Thelwalls, if only in theory, to something about which they knew nothing. 'I told that frightful Leyburn woman that you and I were having the dogs transferred to our joint names and were taking the breed up in partnership.'

His hosts stared at each other and then at him.

'Is this something you two have been cooking up behind my back?' Ruth demanded.

'No, no. David knew nothing about it,' Linus hastened to assure her. 'I know you don't want the bother, and neither do I, for that matter.'

'Then why . . . ?'

'It's difficult to explain,' Linus began. It wasn't difficult at all but it was the sort of thing that, spelled out in plain words, would be hard to believe. 'You see, I've a feeling—well, it's more than a feeling, I'm as sure as I can be—that Morwenna Leyburn and her crew were behind Helen's death.'

They were polite but disbelieving. 'I know there was some animosity between them,' Ruth said, 'and the Leyburn crowd is a very funny lot, but don't you think that's putting it a bit strongly?'

'I know how it sounds,' Linus admitted, 'but I'm fairly sure. I found something in Helen's papers and it ties in with one or two other things. Morwenna obviously hadn't been sure just how strong our—my—commitment to the breed was. Now I've told her. Or at least, I've told her what I want her to think. It should force her hand, don't you think?'

Thelwall looked worried. 'If you've got some evidence, surely you should take it to the police?'

Linus hedged uncomfortably. The Thelwalls were his friends and he had no great wish to mislead them. 'I'm not sure it's evidence in quite that concrete a way,' he said.

'If you're right, do you think it's wise to

"force her hand"?' Ruth asked.

'Perhaps not, but it could give me a more cut and dried case to hand to the authorities in the end,' Linus explained.

'Always assuming you live to do so,' Ruth pointed out. 'After all, if you're right, Helen didn't.'

'I think I'm a bit tougher than Helen.'

Ruth snorted. 'Huh. That comes under the heading of famous last words.'

'What *are* we going to do about the dogs?' David said, anxious to lower the temperature.

'The same as we originally intended, I suppose,' Linus said. 'The trouble is, I think the decent people in the breed have been afraid to come forward because they know they'll incur the wrath of the Leyburn woman if they have the dogs. Once she's out of business it should be plain sailing.'

'You sound very confident,' Thelwall said doubtfully.

'Do I? I'm not. Oh, I'm confident enough that, once she's out of the way, in whatever sense you choose to interpret that expression, her cronies will follow and once that happens there will be several good homes offered where the dogs will be looked after and used to increase the gene pool of the breed which was, after all, Helen's goal. What I'm not so confident about is whether I shall have pushed Morwenna far enough to make her do something she will later regret.'

'Just let's hope you haven't pushed her so far that it's you who regrets it,' Ruth commented.

By tacit consent, the conversation became more general after that and the rest of the evening passed agreeably enough to cause Linus to delay going home until he was afraid it might be beginning to look as if he were after a bed for the night.

He paused in the car park, leaning on the roof of his estate car and admiring the night sky. The forecast had not been good and it was certainly very sultry but it was a beautiful moonlit night. The moon was full but the sky from which it gleamed palely down was not cloudless. Way over in the south-west clouds were forming, humped against the horizon like a range of ancient, time-smoothed hills. A lovely night, but close. If the distant impending storm broke, tomorrow's landscape would be washed clear of atmospheric haze. It would be worth finding a job that took him to the top of a hill tomorrow. Linus climbed into his car and started the engine.

It was on the double bend characteristic of so many Oxfordshire villages that Linus first realized all was not well. His car responded to the clutch but it hadn't slowed as much as he had expected and as a consequence swung too widely round the bends. Linus could only be grateful that nothing had been coming in the opposite direction. It climbed the hill out of the village without any problem and once on the level, Linus, never a driver to take unnecessary risks, tested his brakes. His foot went down to the floor meeting no resistance and with no effect whatsoever upon the car's speed.

His stomach turned over. He glanced at the speedometer. Fifty. An entirely reasonable speed for this stretch of road—when one's brakes were working. He looked in the mirror. There was something behind him. It wasn't any closer than would have been safe, but Linus's brakes weren't working and that meant it was too close especially if the brake lights gave no warning. Linus had no idea whether they went on indicating when the driver's foot was depressing the brake pedal even if the brakes did not respond. If, as he suspected, they didn't, then the following vehicle would probably plough into the back of him, and if he was already ploughing into the back of something else . . . Linus shuddered. It wasn't an appealing prospect. A second glance told him that the vehicle behind wasn't a car. It was some sort of Transit-type of van. Bigger than he was. He changed down into third gear, bracing himself for the jar as the car responded.

The effect of this manoeuvre was short-lived. The road appeared to be level but it was actually sloping very slightly downhill and another glance at the clock soon showed he was back to fifty again.

Linus focused himself to review the road ahead at a faster speed than the car was making. An accident was inevitable. Even in the unlikely event of his getting back to Osney Island without one, he would be unable to pull up in front of his house. He must run the car off the road with as little risk to himself and before he met anything else either travelling more slowly than he in front of him or coming towards him. The man behind would just have to take his chance but at least if Linus drove off into a hedge or ditch, the Transit was unlikely to hit him and, with any luck—though you could never be sure these days—the driver would come over to give him what assistance he could.

There was a bend to the right not far ahead. Not a sharp one but it was edged with a wide, level verge on its left which in turn had a bank and a post-and-rail fence to the field beyond. That was the place. Thank God his steering was all right!

There was still nothing coming towards him but another glance in his mirror told him that the Transit was, if anything, very slightly closer. The road was still sloping imperceptibly downhill and his speed had increased by five miles an hour. The bend was coming up now. Linus put the car into a spine-jarring change to second gear and steered in the straight line that would take him on to the verge and into the bank and fence.

Fifty miles an hour had always seemed a nice, comfortable speed. For the first time in his life Linus realized that a fence coming at you at fifty miles an hour is travelling very fast indeed. He let go of the wheel and instinctively put his arms up to shelter his face as the estate collided with the bank, ran part of the way up it and juddered to a halt with an ear-splitting crack that told him the windscreen had shattered.

He slumped forward towards the steering-wheel but the restraint of his seat-belt held him in a sort of limbo and he instinctively released the catch so that the slump was completed. At the back of his mind he knew he should be getting out of the car but the force of the impact seemed to have left him too limp to move, as if the stuffing had indeed been knocked out of him. He wasn't even aware that the vehicle behind him had drawn up alongside the verge.

He heard the estate door being opened and a man's voice saying, 'You all right, mate?'

He raised his head far enough to allow him to nod and then let it sink again.

'Well, he's not dead yet,' the voice commented. 'Come on, mate. You'd better come with us.'

Linus wasn't sure whether his legs would move and was relieved to find they did, though weakly. The man who had spoken helped him out of the seat and supported him across the verge towards the other vehicle, which Linus noticed without being aware that he had done so was indeed a Transit, painted dark blue and rather crudely customized. He became conscious of a second man who had gone ahead and opened the back of the Transit.

'In you go,' the first one said. 'You'll find a mattress in there. You'll be more comfy like that than sitting in the front with us. OK?'

Linus nodded. It was really very thoughtful of them. Very kind. It restored one's faith in human nature. He found the mattress by a combined use of moonlight and touch and as the doors closed behind him, he noticed that both men had the long hair and unconventional clothes associated, these days, with the so-called peace convoys. Not the sort of people the more conventional citizens associated with such acts of kindness. It just went to show.

They had been driving for a long time before it occurred to Linus to wonder just what it went to show.

If Linus had assumed anything when they helped him into the Transit, it was that he was going to be taken to the Radcliffe Infirmary in Oxford. He had no idea how long they had been travelling but they should surely have been there by now? He raised his left arm to look at his watch and realized that the inside of the Transit was pitch dark. He had been aware of the dark before but had assumed his eyes were still closed. He flicked his eyelids up and down several times. No, his eyes were open. The interior was efficiently blacked out, presumably because it was used for sleeping and this deterred Peeping Toms. It was very difficult to estimate how long he had been in here but even so, he was sure they should have been in Oxford by now.

He sat up gingerly, his stiffening muscles making it a painful exercise. He swivelled round so that he was still sitting on the mattress but had the wall against his back. He needed the support. It is very difficult to judge speed without the existence of stationary objects against which to estimate it, but he didn't think they were going slowly and they were certainly not negotiating many bends. A motorway, then. Perhaps the M40. Maybe they had been on their way to London and, having found Linus wasn't at death's door, decided they didn't have the time to hang around in an Oxford casualty department but would drop him off at a London hospital instead.

No one does that. Linus's common sense was fast reasserting itself. If someone has enough time to go to the assistance of an accident in which the injured party may well be very severely injured, he doesn't quibble at a small detour to take that driver to the nearest hospital. After all, once they'd got him inside the Radcliffe, there would have been no need to stay.

His mind was working better now. Not normally, but better. He was remembering things, too—like the reason for the crash in the first place. His brakes had failed. Odd, that, because there'd been nothing whatever wrong with them during the hundred-mile trip to the show or the hundred miles back. True, Linus knew next to nothing about the internal combustion engine and its associated mechanics. Perhaps brakes did fail quite suddenly from what he could only call natural causes. His own, admittedly limited, previous experience had been of a gradual decline in efficiency and there had been none of that.

He had thought it quite fortunate that this van had been behind him and at a reasonably safe distance. He recalled the two men. He had had an impression that they were both relatively young, and a more definite impression that they came into the category he normally referred to as hippies. Like Morwenna Leyburn's little coterie.

His stomach turned. How long had this vehicle been behind him? He cast his mind back and realized he had no very accurate idea. There had been something behind him for . . . oh, quite a while, but its nature hadn't concerned him until he knew there was danger and he had no idea whether the lights that he now thought he remembered seeing in his mirror had been the same lights all the time or whether there had been more than one vehicle and others had turned off at various places. Wasn't this one dark blue? A colour which disappears at night. It made no difference how hard he thought about it: the transit might have been following him since he left Enstone or it might not. Even if his mind was clear—and it wasn't—he wouldn't have been able to say.

Linus was aware that the Transit was slowing down to swing out into a wide curve to the right and when it straightened out once more, its speed didn't pick up again. There were several gear-changes, a sudden, temporary halt followed by a slow, slightly curving start. Traffic-lights? No. Roundabouts. A town. Possibly one with a by-pass. Linus knew the area well and cast around in his mind to determine where it might be, other than Oxford itself. It was a great disadvantage not to have the slightest idea in which direction they had left the scene of the crash. He didn't think they had been travelling long enough for it to be London and perhaps too long for Northampton to fit the bill. That left Cheltenham or Gloucester, or maybe Swindon. Then there was Newbury or perhaps Reading, though he was inclined to think that, too, was a bit too far. Since he had nothing else to do, he canvassed these ideas, seeking clues in the swaying of the van. He was inclined to favour Newbury and when it headed downhill, braked sharply and turned right before climbing steadily and steeply, he knew he was right. It was not a discovery that got him any further.

There was a stretch of steady, fast driving followed by a more cautious negotiation of some bends and then a sharply downhill section which the van did at some speed and then had to brake hard before turning sharply to the right. It bumped slowly over an uneven surface, stopped, and then reversed before stopping once more. The engine was turned off.

Well, that's that, Linus thought fatuously. We've arrived.

The rear doors of the van were unlocked, which was something of a shock to Linus who hadn't heard them locked in the first place, and they were thrown open.

'OK, mate. We're here now. Out you get.'

Linus struggled to his feet but he was not sufficiently recovered to walk in the necessary stooping position and he tumbled over again. He made it to the doors on his knees.

After so long a time in utter darkness, the moonlight was as disconcerting as sunshine would have been and Linus sat on the tail of the van for a few minutes hoping his eyes would soon become accustomed to the light. The two hippies, one of whom, he now saw, wore his long hair in a pony-tail, gave him a few moments' grace and then pulled him to his feet.

'Think you can walk?' one of them asked.

Linus tried a few steps. His knees felt a bit rubbery but he could walk. 'Yes,' he said. He didn't think he had ever seen either man before.

'D'you think we'd better tie his hands?' one of them asked.

'What for?' the other replied. 'He's not in the best of health now. What do you think he's going to be able to do by the time he gets to the top? *If* he gets to the top.' They glanced away from Linus and both of them laughed.

Linus followed their gaze and realized why they laughed. They were in the rough and ready car park at the foot of Beacon Hill. Linus had no idea how high the hill was but it was a prominent landmark topped by what Linus had always assumed to be Iron Age earthworks. He knew there were several burial mounds in the surrounding fields but he couldn't see them from here. Beacon Hill was one of those places he had always meant to take an hour or so off to climb—there was a well-worn track—but never had. Now it appeared that omission was about to be remedied. Thank goodness it had always looked a fairly gradual incline. Not like Silbury Hill, the man-made mystery where Helen had been found. Silbury wasn't nearly so high but it was much steeper. Even so, if the aim of these men was to induce heart-failure as with Mr Justice Wingfield, they might well succeed. He had been subjected to a succession of unpleasant experiences in the last few weeks; it had been an undoubted shock to discover that his brakes had been tampered with—he no longer wasted any time wondering if it had been accidental. That had been followed by the shock of the crash, to say nothing of the strain of having had to decide to crash deliberately, and now he was going to have to climb Beacon Hill. No, he thought, dispassionately, it wouldn't surprise him at all if he didn't make it—and if he didn't, what then? Would he, too, OD?

He led the way. That way he could at least set the pace.

CHAPTER NINE

There was a field to the right, well-fenced and reaching some way up the lower slopes of the hill. The gate was padlocked and had a notice. Linus guessed it probably announced that the field was private property but as he drew level he saw he was wrong in fact, though probably not in essence. The message read, 'Beware of the Bull,' not a legend one came across very often in these days of bowler-hatted bulls. His professional interest was automatic. He glanced into the pasture and was surprised to see a small herd of Highland cattle. There were about a dozen of them lying down and chewing their cud, the topmost curve of their horns outlined in silver. Linus smiled to himself. Somewhere not too far away was one very canny farmer sleeping the sleep of the just. Joe Public defined a bull as being a cow with horns and usually looked no lower. A field of Highland cows and an old-fashioned notice would be enough to keep trespassers well away. There probably wasn't a bull within miles.

The incline was gradual to start with but, even so, it was uncomfortably steep, given Linus's present condition. He was still setting the pace and his escort seemed content to let him do so but when, after a couple of hundred yards, he paused for breath, a hand on his back propelled him forward.

He soon learned that the appearance of Beacon Hill from the road was deceptive. A fit man might be able to walk up it without the aid of a stick, but it was still a very high, very steep hill—and Linus would never have described himself as fit. The track was easy to follow, thousands of feet having worn the thin topsoil back to the chalk over the years, but wet chalk is slippery and he several times lost his footing and had to put out a hand to prevent a fall. It was often easier to walk to one side of the path, making use of the springy turf, but every so often he had to return to the chalk when a slightly sharper incline forced him to make use of the natural steps, slippery though they might be, worn in the main track.

He was breathing with difficulty now. Beacon Hill could only be a few hundred feet high but Linus felt as if it were Everest. His lungs felt as if they were bursting through his ribcage and when he faltered and was pushed on by his escort, he had too little breath to protest and none at all with which to argue for a respite. By the time he reached the summit, he felt more than half dead and collapsed on top of the concrete trig stone, gasping for breath and only partially aware that someone was waiting for him.

Two people, to be precise. One was a tallish, thickset man in a belted trenchcoat, the collar of which was turned up against the wind that gusted ferociously up here and already smelled as if it had picked up a substantial proportion of the Channel in its uninterrupted course from the south-west. He wore a flat cap pulled down hard over his eyes so that Linus could scarcely make out any features at all, much less identify them. All the same, he felt reasonably sure the man was a complete stranger. There was nothing familiar about his build, his stance or his style, this last seeming quite out of place up here. Trenchcoat notwithstanding, Linus wondered how well fitted the man would be to cope with the impending storm betokened by the clouds now piling up in thick banks against the moon.

The other was Marion Curbridge.

She wore a shapeless raincoat in a darkish, drab shade that was unidentifiable in this light and blended like camouflage against the night sky. It was probably, Linus thought, air force blue. She had crammed on to her head one of those strange waxed hats into which men stick fishing-flies and dog-show women pin club badges. She must have anticipated a probable change in the weather since she carried a furled umbrella of the larger sort carried by golfers. He had difficulty making out her features, too, but no hesitation in identifying her. He said nothing for several minutes, needing his energy to get his breath back.

'You must be just about the last person I expected to see,' he commented at last.

He sensed rather than saw her smile.

'Good,' she said. 'I shouldn't want to be too predictable.'

He glanced at the stranger beside her. 'Your son?' he asked.

'Alas, no. Just someone representing his interest.'

'But you're not going to introduce us.' It was only barely a question.

'A waste of time, I assure you.' She sighed. 'Oh dear, Mr Rintoul, why on earth can't you take a hint and go away?'

Linus tested the strength of the grip holding him on either side and decided there was nothing slack about it. 'If you'd be kind enough to tell these two to let go, I'll be happy to oblige,' he offered.

'Now you know that's not what I meant,' she chided. 'Why did you persist in your involvement with Vampire Dogs? Surely enough was done to discourage you?'

'It was the wrong approach,' he said almost apologetically. 'It was so obviously an attempt to get me out of the breed that I dug my heels in and determined not to go. But I seem to have been wrong about one thing. I thought Morwenna Leyburn was behind it, not you. Or are you simply her representative?'

'Morwenna's representative?' she echoed. 'Good gracious me, no! Why, the woman's as mad as a hatter! Mind you, I can't deny I hoped that was what it would look like and it's mildly gratifying to know that I succeeded to that extent. Oh, she didn't want you in the breed, either, though for very different reasons. I don't care two hoots how many other people have the breed—they're just a hobby for me. Morwenna does. She doesn't want anyone else who might be sufficiently determined in their interest to challenge her position. She just loves being queen bee. That didn't bother me. I wasn't going to flutter round her like some others, but so far as I'm concerned she can get on with it, if that's what she wants. I've even had a couple of Best of Breeds without arousing her ire. A rather tight-lipped smile of congratulation, perhaps, but no ire.'

'And no claque?'

'Now that's one of her more effective techniques. It was directed at Helen, you know. I never experienced it—I never posed a threat, you see.'

Linus frowned, puzzled. 'Then why should either of us matter to you? You've said the breed is just a hobby as far as you're concerned, so why should the presence of either of us in Vampire Dogs upset you so much that you should go to the lengths to which you have gone in order to discourage us? I take it we can thank you for the little dead dogs and the wax figures?'

'Yes, a nice touch that, I thought. Everyone *says* Morwenna's a witch, and I think it's quite probably true, but when it comes to dealing with the competition, I think she generally sticks to whispering campaigns. Her phone bill must be astronomical. By all accounts she hashes and re-hashes shows for days afterwards and I've heard she's a dab hand at the carefully placed phone calls to future judges.'

'But why? You've already said you don't give two hoots who comes into the breed.'

The wind had stopped gusting now and the clouds were so thick that the moon was only occasionally visible. In the unfamiliar stillness the air was unexpectedly oppressive and Linus thought he heard the faint rumble of distant thunder.

'Did I ever tell you I had been married before?' Mrs Curbridge asked.

Linus cast his mind back. Now that she mentioned it, he did have some faint recollection of a remark that intimated as much but he couldn't remember when it had been passed, nor the precise wording. He wasn't even sure it had come from her.

'I seem to have heard something to that effect,' he said. 'Is it relevant?'

'I was Marion Kirkstall then,' she went on, ignoring the question.

Linus frowned. That, too, was familiar but it was something else he couldn't quite place. Except that he didn't think he had heard it in quite the same connection. Then he remembered it was the name of an abbey—in Leeds, he thought. A connection that was of no significance. There was definitely thunder in the distance now. If the storm travelled this way and was a good, strong one, he might be able to make use of its onslaught to escape. He had no idea why he was here or what lay behind the peculiar gathering but he had a very distinct impression it was not to his advantage to linger if he could avoid it.

'Should that name mean something to me?'

he asked.

'It meant something to Helen,' she replied. 'It meant something to Mr Justice Wingfield, too.'

Linus thought he saw the light, or at least part of it: his own connection was still in darkness. 'Has it something to do with the terrorist trial with which they both had a connection?' he asked.

So far as he could tell, she was genuinely puzzled.

'Terrorist trial?' she repeated. 'Were they? I didn't know that. No, the connection was through my son, Matthew Kirkstall.'

Now a small part of the puzzle was beginning to slip into place. It wasn't a ruined abbey that had made the name familiar, but something Helen had said.

'Wasn't he someone Helen had known in Mexico?' he asked.

Mrs Curbridge stiffened and so did the man beside her. 'So she did mention him to you. I thought something must lie behind your interest.'

A few very large drops of rain began to fall and Mrs Curbridge opened her umbrella, its alternating cream and chocolate segments proclaiming Best of Breed and Pedigree Chum respectively. Linus's hopes began to wane. If it was raining already, it suggested that the storm was moving off. He tried to remember what

Helen had told him.

'I remember now,' he said at last. 'Wasn't that the name of the Englishman involved in the scheme to grow marijuana with the help of the irrigation system Peter Glenbarr was putting in? A system which Peter believed was to help food production in a poor country?'

Mrs Curbridge snorted disparagingly. 'He was accused of it, certainly, but he was the only one that was because the others were Mexicans. In fact, as he explained to me, it was the only viable crop up there in the mountains and growing it on a large scale would have brought far more prosperity to the peasants than the crops that woolly-minded sentimentalist, Peter Glenbarr, wanted to see grown. If that interfering busybody hadn't taken his story to the authorities, my Matt would still be with me, instead of languishing in some foul Mexican jail.'

That was probably indisputable but Linus couldn't quite see what it had to do with Helen, and said so. The storm seemed to have changed direction again. The rain had stopped and an occasional flash of lightning from somewhere behind Mrs Curbridge and her still-silent companion was followed after several seconds by the rumble of no-longer-so-distant thunder. Linus's spirits rose. Mrs Curbridge seemed unaware of it, though her companion looked apprehensively over his shoulder once or twice.

'Helen?' she said. 'She egged him on, of course. Matt told me she was the forceful personality in that partnership. It was her idea they should take the Mexican job in the first place. Left to his own impulses, Peter Glenbarr would have accepted the increased salary offered him by Mr Ramirez's father.' She laid a hand on her companion's arm and patted it almost affectionately. 'Well, they got their own back on Peter, of course, but it was too late to help Matthew. There wasn't much I could do about Helen while she remained in Mexico, but once she came back, it was easy—and made all the easier by the peculiarities of Morwenna and her cronies.'

'Couldn't your friend Ramirez have killed her in Mexico for you?' Linus asked.

'Of course he could—and he offered, but I declined. I wanted to make her suffer as much as I had when Matt was arrested, tried and convicted.'

It hadn't apparently occurred to her that the death of her husband might already have caused Helen considerable suffering but Linus guessed it was useless to suggest it. 'And Silbury Hill?' he asked.

She shrugged. 'Window-dressing, that's all. It seems to me you can do two things with a body: either it disappears altogether, which is difficult, or you make it very obvious. Given the Vampire Dog connection and Morwenna's set, any of these pagan sites lead people in that direction and away from normal people, like me.'

That was undoubtedly true, though Linus was beginning to question Mrs Curbridge's normality. 'What has all this do to with me?' he asked.

She seemed surprised. 'You wouldn't have been involved at all if you'd given the dogs up after she died. But you didn't, and you indicated that you were going to root around until you'd found out what it was all about, and I couldn't have that, now could I?'

'No,' Linus said. 'Put like that, I suppose not.' The thunder and lightning were closer together now and Mr Ramirez was distinctly jumpy. Linus was aware, too, of sudden tensions in the men who held him every time the firmament split temporarily asunder. Mrs Curbridge was unmoved by it all. There was still one piece missing. 'Where did Wingfield fit in to all this?' he asked.

'Mr Justice Wingfield always dealt notoriously severely with people up before him on charges connected with drugs.'

'Quite possibly, but your son was tried in Mexico, which hardly comes under a British judge's authority.'

'When Matt was arrested, we tried to persuade the Mexican authorities just to deport him. Even though that would have left a shadow over his name, he would have been free. As it happened, Wingfield was in Mexico at the time at some sort of legal convention discussing what was best to be done over the whole narcotics issue, and he came down heavily against it—even though it was not strictly any of his business. He said that law-breakers should stand trial in the country where they broke the law and if the penalties were severe, well—tough. Then, when Matt had been convicted, we tried to get him brought back to serve his sentence here. Wingfield was very loud in his insistence that it wasn't legally possible and that undoubtedly influenced the decision to leave him where he was.'

'Maybe he was quite simply right,' Linus suggested.

'Don't be stupid,' Mrs Curbridge snapped. 'Matt's bosses have influence in very high places. If Wingfield hadn't made such a public song and dance about it, Matt might well have been brought back. No, he deserved to die. We'd intended he should be given an OD too—that way, he'd have been thoroughly discredited, but he turned out to have a weak heart. That's what gave me the idea of making it look *really* weird. Until then, I hadn't really thought of making use of the dog connection but it worked rather well. A stroke of genius, one might say, especially since Helen was also involved with dogs.'

'I suppose you went into the breed deliberately to get closer to her,' Linus suggested.

'Goodness me, no. That was pure coincidence. I'd had them for two or three years before she came back to England. I hadn't realized we shared an interest. It just made everything easier.'

'So what happens now? To me, I mean.'

Mrs Curbridge opened her mouth to speak but her first words were drowned in a clap of thunder accompanied by an almost simultaneous flash of lightning. She peered up round the edge of her umbrella. 'My,' she said, 'if we're not quick we're going to be drenched. We've had an unplanned heart attack and an overdose of heroin so this time it will be something a bit different. Did you have a proper autopsy on the little corpse I sent you?'

'Yes. Curare.'

'That's right. The Amazonian connection again, you see. Brings it all back to the dogs and Morwenna.'

'Not as easy to get hold of, though.'

'Very true, but Mr Ramirez's father is a most obliging man and Matthew has been *so* discreet about their connection—to the point of blankness, one might say.' She turned to her companion. 'Have you got it, Juan?'

The man in the trenchcoat brought out a hyperdermic syringe and carefully removed the protective cover from the needle. He shook his head. 'I don't like all this subtlety,' he said. His accent was that of a man who had been taught English by Americans.

'If it's curare,' Linus remarked—as much to gain time as for any interest in the answer—'you must have had some difficulty getting hold of it.'

Juan Ramirez looked at him pityingly. 'You can get hold of anything if you're prepared to pay for it,' he said. 'In this case, though, I brought it with me.'

'I'm flattered you went to the trouble—and surprised it wasn't detected.'

'Don't kid yourself—I haven't come all this way just to get rid of you,' the Mexican said scornfully. 'I'm here to spearhead our British operation and Mrs Curbridge has been kind enough to offer assistance. She'll be as well remunerated for that as her son is for his silence. Anything else we can do for her is a little bonus. None of us like people nosing into our affairs. Curare has its uses—not least the fact that no one's hooked on it so no one's looking for it.' He glanced towards the two men holding Linus. 'Ready?' he said.

'The jugular vein would be poetic justice,' Mrs Curbridge commented.

Ramirez grinned. 'Wouldn't it just? Hold him hard.'

Linus's escort did just that, and as the

Mexican approached him Linus's faith in divine retribution, previously never very strong, experienced a surge in power as there came from immediately overhead a deafening roar of thunder and with it simultaneously the dark sky was split in two by a jagged flash that descended to earth, homing in with unerring accuracy to the highest point in the landscape: the umbrella's long metal tip. It ran down the shaft to the wooden handle, which shattered to the accompaniment of the most blood-curdling scream Linus had ever heard, all the more disconcerting because it came from Mrs Curbridge's throat. The cry ceased as abruptly as it had begun and she crumpled to the ground. The attention of the three men was temporarily diverted from Linus and the hold on his arms slackened.

This was the opportunity he had been hoping for, if more dramatic than he had expected. He seized it, tore himself free of the loosened hold and flung himself down the track, his very speed unbalancing him but some miracle keeping him on his feet.

He heard the shout that greeted the realization of his escape but wasted no time looking behind him. There was another burst of thunder with the simultaneous lightning-flash that indicated the storm was directly overhead.

Then it rained.

The clouds emptied a veritable deluge over

the downland, sheets of water that drenched him to the skin in seconds, totally obscured the way ahead and must mercifully make it impossible for any pursuers to see him. Such a downpour would be short-lived. He headed off the track at a tangent towards the north, recollecting the field of Highland cattle that must be a short cut to the car park. Now the running was harder: the incline was steeper, the short, springy downland grass as slippery now as ever the chalk track had been, but he kept going. He had no choice. The car park. If there was a drivable car, fine. If not, then on to the main road. Surely someone would take pity on a poor half-drowned pedestrian?

Another flash of lightning which followed a few seconds later told him the storm was moving on. He thought he detected a shout behind him. He had reached the pasture fence now and scrambled between two of the strands of barbed wire, ripping his coat sleeve but barely noticing it. For the first time he looked back. The three men were closer than he had expected, even Ramirez in his citified salutation to country clothes. They must have anticipated his short cut.

The cattle were on their feet, the storm making them restless. The unfamiliar sight of a running man increased their unease and, as Linus passed, he realized that the farmer's notice had not been bluff. A very mature head of horns swayed from side to side, its ring clearly visible, and Linus swerved to avoid it.

Highland cattle are placid beasts but a storm and a charging lunatic are enough to upset the most benign of animals, and when that first lunatic had passed and others approached, the bull had had enough. Linus raced on and vaulted with an expertise he had never displayed at school over the gate at the far end. He heard a scream and glanced back in time to see a figure hurled through the air. The bad visibility made it impossible to determine which of the three it had been. Linus hoped Ramirez was the victim because he had a shrewd suspicion the other two, being presumably nothing more than hired English thugs, would cut their losses and run. Whoever it was, no one stopped to help him, whether from fear of the bull or anxiety to catch Linus. The wind was behind him now that he was nearly at the car park and he heard a shout from behind. The man's voice was familiar and although most of the words were blown away, he thought he made out '. . . the keys . . .'

Linus ran across the uneven hardcore of the car park. He would try the Transit. If he had misheard, it would have to be the road. They were too close to risk trying either of the other two cars he now noticed parked there, one of them a fast, sleek job, the other presumably Mrs Curbridge's.

His hunch that it was the Transit proved correct. They had left it unlocked. The driver's door slid back at a touch and Linus's heart leapt with pure joy. His ears had not deceived him. The idiots had left the keys in the ignition. God bless all idiots!

He climbed in, pulled the door across and locked it. He turned the key. Pray God there's plenty of petrol, he implored. A face, long and drenched, appeared at the window. One of his abudctors. The engine turned. Linus let in the clutch, selected a gear at random and released the brake. The face disappeared as he headed for the road.

He had a mind-shattering wait of thirty seconds that felt like thirty years to let someone else go past before he could turn on to the highway and his mirror told him that someone had turned out behind him. He knew he must lack both the speed and the acceleration of either of the other two cars but he rather thought that, if it came to the crunch—an unfortunate expression in the circumstances—he had the tougher vehicle.

Linus put his foot down. The Transit responded sluggishly and the uphill slope was not the best stretch of road to test its pace, so he wasn't surprised when a car drew level and stayed level with him until the dual-carriageway ended, when it pulled ahead and slowed down. It was the sports car and there were two men in it. The driver was Ramirez.

The manoeuvre had been transparent enough. He had realized precisely what was being attempted but his own vehicle's speed coupled with a gradient that was just sufficient to hinder the sort of acceleration he had at his disposal, prevented his doing anything to forestall it.

Linus was a law-abiding driver, considerate by nature and polite by training. He slowed down to avoid bumping into Ramirez's car. The stretch of road ahead was straight and level now for a couple of miles, perhaps more. One of those stretches on which it is possible to travel quite fast if there is nothing slower in front, but not really wide enough to allow overtaking unless there is no oncoming traffic. Unfortunately, there was.

Linus found himself slowing down more and more as Ramirez decelerated. A glance in his mirror told him there was another car behind him. It might be anyone who just happened to be using the A34 that night. It might not. In the nature of Ramirez's business he was likely to have either a radio or a car-phone by means of which reinforcements could easily have been summoned. It was entirely possible he was hemmed in. He moved over towards the middle of the road, staying in his lane but keeping his eye on the opposite one ahead. He saw the light of an approaching car, the distortion of the rain and the reflections from the wet road making it difficult to gauge its speed. Never mind. There were times when risks were worth taking.

He stepped hard on the accelerator, bracing himself against the collision with Ramirez's car. It was harder than he had anticipated and took him longer to make a recovery but it must have been a total shock to the unprepared Ramirez, who had, Linus hoped, been lulled by his previous lack of initiative.

He pulled the wheel hard to the right and accelerated to whip past the faster vehicle before the oncoming car was close enough to hit him but sufficiently near to deter Ramirez from accelerating immediately. His instinct for his own survival should be to hang back until the apparent danger was past. If he did so, it would give Linus several useful seconds before the more responsive car could close the gap and this time, when it did, he should be able to prevent its overtaking by swerving from side to side. That was the theory.

It worked. He faced a barrage of honks and flashing lights from the approaching car whose driver must have thought his end had come, and Linus bore him no grudge for that. He steered back into his own lane and pulled away as quickly as he could.

He kept the crown of the road, the more easily to block any attempt to pass him. Ramirez was soon on his tail again but his strategy was successful, enabling him to keep in front of the Mexican no matter on which side he tried to overtake. Linus was too close for comfort to the approaching traffic, which was infrequent but fast, and he scarcely noticed the horn blasts, so intent was he upon the job in hand.

Now they were reaching the curving downhill approach to the roundabout south of Newbury. The left-hand turn at the bottom was sharp and dangerous at any speed beyond a walking pace and Linus had a feeling that if he braked at speed at the same time as turning sharply to the left, he might very well simply spin in a circle and stop—if he were lucky. He was no stunt driver. He was going to have to risk losing some of his present advantage and hope he could hold Ramirez off on the slow uphill incline after the roundabout.

He knew he was still going too fast as the last few yards raced towards him and now he spotted the added complication of an army convoy heading towards the roundabout from Newbury. If they were turning south on the A34, it could be very sticky.

As the army's presence registered, so did the fact that Ramirez was pushing past him on the turn. He was abreast of him now, and his sheer speed could only send him so wide round the turn that he could hardly fail to hit the convoy. Linus pulled over to the left and stood on his brakes as the Transit jerked on to the grass and its nearside wing crunched into a road sign that slowed it to a halt before expiring.

Linus saw Ramirez's car race past him in a wide arc that carried it inexorably into a collision with one of the heavy military lorries. The convoy had not been travelling fast but the nature of the vehicles made quick evasive action impossible and Ramirez's speed was sufficient to guarantee that the impact was massive and conclusive.

The lorry was slightly damaged. Ramirez and his passenger could hardly have survived.

The army reacted quickly. The road was now completely blocked and the officer in charge stationed outposts on all the access roads to the roundabout to advise drivers to make a detour. Someone radioed for the emergency services and a shaken Linus heard a tapping on the Transit window. He remembered that he had locked himself in, and released the catch. The soldier standing there slid the door back.

'You all right, mate?' he asked. 'Can you move?'

Linus tried. He could.

The soldier reached across and unfastened the seat-belt which Linus had no recollection of having fastened in the first place. It must have been instinct. 'Come on,' the man said. 'Let's get you somewhere safer than this.'

He steadied Linus's shaky descent from the

Transit and a colleague ran across the road with a heavy army blanket in which he enveloped him. They led him over to one of their vehicles and sat him down on the step.

'The ambulance'll be here in a minute,' a voice said, and someone produced the top of a vacuum flask and handed it to Linus. It was full of hot, sweet tea.

'The other car,' Linus said. 'Is it . . . are they . . . ?'

''Fraid so. Didn't stand a chance. No need for you to worry, though. He was driving like a lunatic. Drunk, probably. Mind you, you weren't exactly driving slowly yourself, but the accident was entirely the other chap's fault. Must have been mad to try to overtake on that bend. Don't blame yourself.'

Linus didn't answer. He hugged the plastic cup in both hands and sipped. It was still raining, though the torrential force of a short time before had abated, but the thick blanket kept the wet at bay.

The police and the ambulancemen arrived simultaneously and put Linus in a police car while the army's diagnosis on Ramirez and his passenger was confirmed. A constable took Linus's details.

'Inspector Lacock,' Linus said. 'Is he here? Or Detective-Inspector Netley?'

'No, sir. No reason why they should be, is there? The army's told us what happened. It'll take us a bit of time to identify the other two, of course, but it shouldn't be too difficult. I don't expect it'll be a CID job and Newbury can cope with the accident. No need to send to HQ.' He used the patient tone appropriate for dealing with someone who was clearly in shock.

'I can identify the driver,' Linus said. 'At least, I know the name he was using. He's a Mexican—Juan Ramirez. His father's something big on the drugs scene.'

'That's very interesting, sir,' the constable said non-committally, but he unobtrusively beckoned another policeman over to stay with Linus while he sought out his superior.

'I understand you know the driver?' that officer said.

Linus nodded. 'Juan Ramirez—at least that's the name he's using. Can you contact Inspector Lacock?'

'I can, and Detective-Inspector Netley, but I'd need a good reason for doing so.'

Linus managed a wry smile. 'No problem,' he said. 'Up there on Beacon Hill you'll find a woman who's been struck by lightning. Almost certainly dead, I should think, though I didn't stop to find out. Marion Curbridge, formerly Kirkstall. Her son, Matthew, is in a Mexican jail on drugs offences. The driver of that car is the son of the man who organizes it all. Mrs. Curbridge is behind two recent deaths—Helen Glenbarr's and Mr Justice Wingfield's. They both had connections with the son's case. The Ramirezes were behind the death in Mexico of Mrs Glenbarr's husband. It's all a bit complicated,' he added apologetically.

At the mention of the judge's name there was a tenseness in the air that had been quite absent before when the only thing under consideration had been a nasty but apparently straightforward road accident.

'I see, sir.' Linus wasn't entirely sure the man believed him, but he could hardly blame him for that. The inevitable blood-test would at least prove he wasn't drunk. 'In that case,' the officer went on, 'you won't mind coming along with us, will you? Constable—' he turned to the younger man—'get a message to HQ, will you? You'd better mention Lacock and Netley.' He turned back to Linus. 'Happy now, sir?'

Linus closed his eyes in exasperation and fatigue.

'Deliriously,' he said.

Photoset, printed and bound in Great Britain by
REDWOOD PRESS LIMITED, Melksham, Wiltshire